The Princess in Black!

The Princess in Black!

An unheard story of Mughals

Upendra Dharmadhikari

•

Changali Anand

Srishti
Publishers & Distributors

SRISHTI PUBLISHERS & DISTRIBUTORS
N-16, C. R. Park
New Delhi 110 019
editorial@srishtipublishers.com

First published by
Srishti Publishers & Distributors in 2014

All characters in this book are fictitious, and any resemblance to real persons, living or dead, is coincidental.

The authors assert the moral right to be identified as the authors of this work.

Printed and bound in India

A tribute to Late Shri Dwarka Nath Dharmadhikari,
my grandfather, who taught me basics of storytelling
– Upendra Dharmadhikari

To my Noor, Vidya
– Changali Anand

Prologue

Echoes of a horse's gallop ring loud and clear through the still jungle. Birds perched on trees shift their necks, to the left, to the right. The pristine body of a deer, at full stretch, bursts through the faded foliage. The horse powers its stride in close pursuit. Trees and leaves of the forest, coloured brown covered in winter's decay, are mute spectators.

A sharp, bearded face leans closer to the stallion's ears; the master whispers silent encouragements.

The horse and its bearded master were part of a pack following a herd of deer. The master had set his sights and followed his target. The deer broke away from its herd; master and steed broke away from their pack.

The steed increases its pace; autumn leaves resting gently on the ground are blown away. The deer falls in sight of the man commanding his stallion. He steadies his torso, draws his arrow on the bow, taut, and releases it. The pointed tip slices through the silent air. Instincts of the deer warn it to change its course; its body deftly moves mid-air and the arrow misses its mark. A frown flashes on the face of the hunter.

Unknown to the huntsman, he is in the sight of another hunter: a natural predator ready to strike from the trees above. Black spots on golden skin glitter in the sun; the eyes of the leopard are firmly fixed on man and horse tearing through the floor of the forest. As the man strings another arrow, the leopard leaps from the tree.

The hands of time slow down: The hunter catches the leopard from the corner of his eye, image of the predator grows large on the rider's pupils, but he cannot move, he cannot react. The leopard's body crashes into rider and stallion, and for a brief moment, hunter and prey are united. White, brown, and yellow – bodies of horse, leopard, and man – roll on the ground providing colour and hue to the grey forest.

The rider gets up quickly, bits and pieces of brown foliage stuck in his elegant, bottle green robe. His white stallion lies motionless on the ground, the stillness of death about to set in. He tightens his grip on his sword, staring at the predator. The gaze of the rider is that of no ordinary man, but an emperor who will establish a dynasty that will be remembered through the annals of time.

The laws of the jungle, however, do not distinguish between emperor and commoner. You either hunt, or get hunted. Eyes of the leopard see just a man, a target that needs to be hunted down. It leaps forward. The rider does not hold back; he lunges forward removing his metal blade from its sheath.

The beast digs its paws into the leg of the bearded man, spooning flesh with its claws, drawing first blood. The rider grimaces, stifling his scream, blocking his pain, and slashes his metal blade across the paw of the beast. A swift straight cut gashes on its paw. The predator growls and takes a step back. Down on one knee, blood oozing out dripping like pins on the floor of the forest, the rider breathes long and hard trying to focus. He looks up only to see the leopard at arm's length, ready to strike him down once again.

A bright white flash illuminates the scene.

It blinds the leopard temporarily. The bearded rider quickly shields his eyes, his hunter's instinct drives him to sinks his sword into the gut of the animal a few heartbeats away. The leopard staggers and falls down; the silver blade embedded deep inside its gut.

The hunter falls on his back.

Still covering his eyes, the rider tries to identify the source of light, a light which saved his life. He observes a palm-sized diamond lying next to him shining brightly. The angle of the afternoon sun had hit the precious stone and illuminated it like a full moon.

He could not believe it. The stone he always carried with him had created a future when his present seemed a finite end. His left hand, smudged red with blood, grasps the big stone. The bright light fades, with a hue of red; the man's eyelids drooped.

In the distance, a faint rustle is heard. His eyes struggle open. The rustle grows louder and nears the rider. The man summons his will and stands his weakening body up. If this is another threat, he is ready to deal with it. The man, Babur, knew he was destiny's child.

A white robe sashays amidst the faded foliage; naked feet walk to the victorious hunter; a gentle voice enquires of the bleeding man, "Are you all right, my son?"

1

A soft smile spread on Professor Narayan Shastri's face. The brightest student in his class had said Dabur instead of Babur, the first Mughal Emperor.

Gentle laughter echoed across the wide walls of the classroom, which was sparsely occupied. History was not a popular subject for the present generation whose attention span was equivalent to the time it took to cook instant noodles. A motley group of students were in attendance on a cold, winter morning for their lecture with pullovers and shawls, the dress code of the morning. The long windows of the classroom were shut tightly in an attempt to keep the cold out and preserve any warmth the walls of the room held.

The bumbling student, a girl, flushed beet red. *A Freudian slip perhaps...*Narayan noted to his own self.

Just a week ago, Dabur had sponsored a history quiz competition at Delhi University. Though the subject was not a popular one, the quiz had drawn many participants and a sizeable audience largely due to the presence of a Hindi film actor who was the chief guest of the event present to promote his film, a historical, which was releasing soon.

Narayan continued to smile. Small moments like these reaffirmed the professor's belief that he had done the right thing by staying back. He had turned down an offer to teach Indian history at the prestigious Princeton University a couple of years ago. His exhaustive research on an ancient manuscript penned by Bahadur Shah Zafar had made him a rising star in the field of Historical Studies. The research paper contested that the manuscript contained a chemical equation, in code, to a potent weapon which could help an army win a losing battle in an instant. The idea was met with open ridicule as well as overwhelming praise.

Narayan, with his intellectual but eye-pleasing personality, soon found himself to be the face of Historical Studies – an academic vertical which carried the baggage of being scholarly and boring. Narayan adjusted the frame of his spectacles.

2

Captain Veer Pratap Singh paced restlessly around Professor Narayan Shastri's cabin. He maintained a strict posture with his black blazer buttoned on. A high-ranking official at the Defence Intelligence Agency (DIA), he was used to instant obedience. The fact that a history professor had the nerve to put his agenda on hold irritated him.

The slow winter sun flooded the cabin with its warm light, revealing its features. Large historical tomes comfortably crowded the room on bookshelves built into its walls. Wherever the eyes rested, there was always a book in sight. Books seemed to be the motif of the room's décor. The books were arranged in alphabetical manner and placed neatly into the shelves. Some of them were faded, some of them mint fresh; some of them had narrow vertical lines running the length of their spines, some of them seemed untouched, almost all of them were related to history. Not a single book was out of place, leading Captain Veer to wonder whether these books were merely to impress visitors.

An intricately carved mahogany desk sat in the centre of the room with four cushioned chairs for company. The chairs were wide and sat tall. Major Avinash Singh Rathore occupied one of the cushioned chairs. The officer sat in a relaxed manner, with his navy-blue blazer unbuttoned, a hint of belly fat straining against the fabric of his white shirt. He placed his hand on the desk where the winter sun created a triangle and allowed his hand to bask in its warmth. Images of a child warming his hand on a bright triangular pie of sunshine on a brick wall flashed through the memory of the officer. As a child, Major Rathore had known no better feeling than to chase the warmth of the sun on a cold winter day.

The mundane academic decor of the room was broken with a centre piece that was all the rage a few decades ago: Two birds, elongated and cylindrical in shape, dipping their beaks in and out of a cup. The base of the two birds contained a particular liquid that acted as counterweights causing the objects to move back and forth, back and forth.

As Major Rathore glanced across the room, he observed one historical tome after another lining the shelf: *A People's History of the World*, *Liberation: The Bitter Road to Freedom*, *India After Gandhi*: *The History of the World's Largest Democracy*, *The Canonical Discovery of India*. One book, however, caught his attention – *The Art of War* by Sun Tzu. The officer wondered why a book on military strategies occupied a place among its historical peers. It was clearly the odd man out.

Captain Veer continued to pace across the room, his hands crossed behind his back.

"Calm down...," Major Rathore chided his partner.

Captain Veer's eyes growled.

"Okay...have it your way," Major Rathore backed off.

Captain Veer had developed a sense of acute irritability towards people who did not follow orders. He wanted to talk to the professor regarding a matter of national security and the man had nonchalantly put him on hold. "Everyone behaves like a politician nowadays," muttered the Captain to himself.

The tall, athletic figure of Professor Narayan Shastri strode past the empty corridor. He was wearing a comfortable v-neck pullover paired with navy blue trousers, well-tailored. Multicoloured posters, notices, Dabur print ads from the quiz competition, and the occasional cobweb tangling gingerly on ignored corners of the corridor walls greeted the professor. He had immediately recognized the tone of the visitor who stopped by his class earlier. Having an army man for a father, Narayan had been raised on a strict diet of discipline and paying obeisance to authority. It was only as a young adult that Narayan began to question his father's authority in a monk-like manner and stand his ground. He knew how to tackle people who expected the world to follow their spoken word without delay: with a mixture of patience and indifference.

The doorknob of the cabin turned and creaked open. Captain Veer stopped in his stride and looked at the professor, "Do you really think that a matter of national security is more important than a roomful of students who are high on hormones and acne?"

The officer's voice rang across the small room like a raging bull.

Narayan took a deep breath and let it out slow, "One of two things can happen. Either you tell me what the matter of national importance is...or I could walk out of this door and leave you two gentlemen to enjoy the rest of your day here at Delhi University."

A tense moment of silence followed. The two birds continued to move back and forth, back and forth, on the desk.

"Professor Shastri, hello...I am Major Avinash Singh Rathore. This is my partner, Captain Veer Pratap Singh. We are from the Defence Intelligence Agency, DIA if you like...," the words pierced the silent air, creating a much needed interjection.

"Hi. Call me Narayan, please," Prof. Shastri smiled and took a few steps towards his seat.

"What brings you guys here?" Narayan sunk into his chair and faced the two officers.

Captain Veer continued to glare at the professor. His partner tapped a few buttons on his mobile touch screen. A sharp image of an ancient object flashed on screen. Narayan's eyes lit up at the image, reflecting a mix of wonderment and suspicion.

"This is why we have come to you," said Captain Veer, a hint of anger trailed his voice.

3

Narayan ran his fingers across his smooth, clean-shaven chin. His eyes, gazing past the window, reflected a pensive state of mind.

What he had heard from the DIA officers worried him. The ancient artefact flashing on the mobile screen, had been stolen yesterday night. It was kept on view at Purana Qila's Museum. Nothing much was known about this artefact, except that it was discovered at a recent archaeological survey conducted on the outskirts of New Delhi.

An intuition rising from his gut told Narayan that trouble was just a step away.

"Apart from the fact that the artefact has been stolen, what really bothers us is the presence of Major Salim Khan," Major Rathore interrupted Narayan's silent contemplation.

"Pardon my ignorance, but who is Major Salim Khan?" asked Narayan still gazing out of the window.

"All that you need to know is that he is an enemy of our state," replied Captain Veer, a hint of irritation trailed his voice.

"Veer…," Major Rathore glanced at his partner, "I think the professor ought to know the details."

Veer pursed his lips and clasped his hands tightly.

Major Rathore turned to face Prof. Shastri, "Professor, Major Salim Khan was a key member of the ISI; a young army officer who rose quickly up its ranks. What you achieved in your field of Historical Studies, Salim Khan did with Pakistan Intelligence. His ability to manipulate the west and exploit any resource available for the benefit of the ISI endeared him to his seniors and the chief of the agency."

Narayan nodded, slowly soaking in the information.

"He left the ISI following the death of his sister, whom he was very close to. She was a part of a cultural exchange program from a college in London that toured Delhi last year. Unfortunately, she was killed in the blasts."

The professor leaned forward in rapt attention.

"To cut a long story short, Salim Khan suffered a nervous breakdown, retired from the ISI, and dropped off the radar."

"Hmm…," Narayan exhaled.

Major Rathore continued, "For a man who had disappeared from public memory, it is surprising that he should resurface at Purana Qila's Museum a few days ago."

"This is what he looks like," Captian Veer jumped into the conversation. He flashed his mobile screen to professor Shastri. The professor could make out an imposing figure at the left hand corner of the screen. His eyes stayed on the figure, but soon shifted to the beaming smile of a young girl covering the major part of the screen.

"Who is this?" he enquired.

"Nobody…just stay on the topic," Captain Veer snapped.

"It's his daughter," replied Major Rathore smiling.

Narayan's eyebrows rose; he did not peg the Captain to be a doting father of a beaming child.

"Sir…does he need to know everything?"

"And exactly what am I supposed to help you with?" interrupted Narayan, speaking in a subdued tone.

"Your expertise on the Mughal Dynasty could help us trace a connecting line between the theft and the presence of the retired Major. Besides, you come highly recommended…," trailed Major Rathore's voice.

Narayan got up from his chair, walked to a nearby bookshelf, and picked up a book – *Alberuni's India*.

"By whom?"

"Your father, Lieutenant General Madan Shastri…"

The professor froze.

A kid comes flying on a shiny new bicycle, his tender hands try to control the handle, the wheels swerve and lift off the ground; the blue bicycle crashes. Dust settles around his shredded pair of jeans, which blot stains of blood. The kid looks to his father seated upright on a bench nearby. The boy half expects his father to walk to him and help him up, offering words of comfort. The man continues to sit on the bench and says, "When we fall down, we must pick ourselves up. Now, get up."

A shiny new trophy in hand, a teenager hugs his mom and grins ear to ear. This has been one of the best days of his life. The father simply remarks, "What's the big deal… you came third in a quiz competition; two places behind the winner. Might as well not have won at all."

A young man studies diligently, burning the midnight oil. Pages of a history book turn slowly creating a slow echo. "Narayan is not going to make anything of his life if he continues his foolish pursuit of studying the past," his father's voice rings through the silent night. The young man shuts out the voice, as he had been doing all through his life, and continues with the book.

"Narayan…Mr. Shastri…" The professor's mind rushed back to the present. Everything was a blur. He tried to focus on the pages of a book he had just picked up. He looked at the two men and simply stared at them. Narayan wanted to say something, but he could not articulate.

"Is everything all right?" Major Rathore enquired with a hint of concern.

"No, it is not." Narayan slid the book back into the shelf, and made his way, slowly, to the chair and sat down. "You say my father, Lieutenant General Shastri, recommended me?"

The two men nodded.

"I find that hard to believe."

"Why would we lie to you?" shot back Captain Veer. He looked at his partner, "Sir…let's go. I think we are wasting our time here."

"We have been in constant touch with your father since the intelligence department alerted us about Major Salim Khan yesterday," the calm voice of Major Rathore intervened. "When we told him that Object No. 27 had gone missing, he told us to get in touch with you immediately."

Narayan rocked back and forth in his chair. The two plastic birds on his desk too rocked back and forth.

He still could not believe what he was hearing. *Why would a man who never believed in me suddenly recommend me*...deliberated Narayan.

"Narayan...we are running short on time. Could you please help us?" Major Rathore implored.

Narayan bent forward and rubbed his hands together, "Yes."

"Great!" The Major immediately brought forth a high-resolution colour photograph of the missing ancient artefact – Object No. 27. It was dated 2 July 2007.

The professor scanned the image; his eyes immediately caught sight of an ancient script embedded on the object. He leapt out of his chair and rushed towards the bookshelf. A child-like energy overcame Narayan. Captain Veer Pratap eyed him curiously.

Narayan took out a voluminous book and gently blew the dust away from its hard cover. The dust sizzled and shimmied in the streaming sunlight. He quickly turned the pages of the book, with the photograph in one hand. He stopped on a particular page; his index finger moved right to left on the page. His fingers stopped midway, "Jaa keh....der.... ha bh... shedh."

Major Rathore and Captain Veer tried to follow Narayan's alien-like mutterings but could not decipher it. The professor rushed back and began to scribble on the writing pad placed on his desk. The eyes of the two officers followed him closely.

Narayan scribbled on his writing pad, looked at it, and slouched on his chair. He calmly looked out of the window into the distance.

Seconds ticked away.

"Do you need an invitation to speak?" Veer was growing restless.

"A place where I read in the light of stars," said the professor continuing to gaze out of the window. "This script here in the photograph," Narayan pointed it out to the two officers, "It is Farsi. Roughly translated, it reads: A place where I read in the light of stars."

"Does it signify anything?" enquired Major Rathore.

The professor rubbed his chin with his right hand. He was trying to course the maze of all the information he possessed and give a valid explanation.

"Satyamev...satyamev...satyamev jayate..." The quiet solitude of the room was broken. Veer quickly took out his phone, "This is Captain Veer Pratap. Yes...yes...are you sure?" His eyes lit up. "Ok, we are on our way."

Veer looked at his partner and Narayan, "Time to go."

4

Soft, orange rays of the afternoon sun streamed in gently through the large opaque windows and flooded the room like a warm greeting. An emerald-green object stood perfectly still in the centre of the wide, rectangular room, safely encased behind a glass case. Though other relics occupied the same room, the emerald-green object was an eye-catcher: the sparking pole star on a new moon night.

A soft shadow was cast on the dull, orange-coloured walls of the room; a pair of anklets rustled as a graceful, feminine figure took half a step forward. Dressed in a warm winter jacket paired with crisp blue denims and an embroidered woollen scarf draped around her head, she was the sole representative of the present in a room filled with the past. A black shoulder bag with a diamond imprint was her sole companion. Her deep, brown eyes stopped and stared at the triangle-shaped object. It was breathtaking. Gazing at the object, she felt the hands of time running her life stop and rest for a while as her eyes took in its enrapturing magnificence. *Neither the most poetic of descriptions nor the clearest of images could capture this aura*, she mused.

A rush of words began filling up her conscious mind. She felt like a writer in the first flush of a muse's inspiration. An irresistible need to write her thoughts down pulsed through her. Out came her journal and pen from her knapsack. As soon as the pen touched the blank page of her journal, it began to scribble words.

Lost in her pages, sharp echoes of approaching footsteps were muted to her.

A portly figure entered the room and walked with a sense of acquired authority and indifference. Cracks ran from the soles to the flat head of the shoe displaying signs of the weight it bore from day-to-day. The figure swayed and moved, dark red beetle juice stain marking the lower-lip a vermilion line neatly dividing the wrinkled forehead, and stepped to the glass case. The eyes shifted around furtively, looking left and then right; it sighted the presence of the young woman who was lost deep in a transcendental word. Her hands moved at the speed of sound, writing. Assured there was no threat, his eyes returned to the case. A metallic jingle escaped into the silent air, which swallowed it immediately like a hungry beast. Laser-cut keys punched the empty air, as the sunlight ran off its edges, and entered its inherited slot just below the transparent container. The glass case slid open. Calm, steady fingers reached out and grasped the emerald-green object. The glass case slid close, the figure walked away just as it had entered the room: with a sense of indifference.

A minute hand moved at its own pace on an ancient wall clock hanging in the room.

She stopped writing; it seemed as if an alarm bell had gone off in her head. Her eyes darted around, looking for a missing piece in the puzzle. And then it struck her: the empty glass cage. Numbness soaked her entire body and held it firmly in its grasp.

A vacuum had been created in the room; its most prized possession had disappeared in a blink, as if a magician had just performed his greatest act.

The big, round tower clock had its short hour hand at VIII and long minute hand at VI; the time read 8:30. A white sedan zipped through the crisp, morning air. Rathore was driving the car, Captain Veer sat on the passenger seat with his eyes glued on his smart phone; Narayan occupied the rear seat, watching the concrete road rush by his eyes as if it were a flowing stream.

The capital city was slowly stirring into life: old men and women went about their daily walks swinging their arms to and fro without a care in the world, snug in their brown coloured vests and monkey caps; young men and women ran or jogged trying to outpace one another, snug in their black sweatshirts and leg warmers with white earphones dangling to fro from their necks without a care in the world. Soft droplets of steam wafted out of their nostrils and mouths as the men and women ran or walked.

For an instant, Narayan wondered whether the young and old had their particular colour code.

The professor's eyes and ears were on the road but his mind was ticking away, trying to figure out the meaning behind the script he had seen on Object No. 27. A visual map popped up inside the professor's head with the faces of Babur, Humayun, Akbar, Jahangir, Shah Jahan, and Aurangzeb. *A place where I read in the light of stars...maybe a place connected to reading and stars, or could it be a metaphor for a throne, for a kingdom.* The professor's mind ticked away. *Babur, Jahangir, Aurangzeb...none of these emperors had a reading habit or a star gazing one. Stars...read...Akbar, Shah Jahan...no, dead end. Humayun...read...library...stars...Purana Qila... Sher Mandal. That's it, Sher Mandal.*

A content smile appeared on the professor's face. *Good...* Narayan muttered to himself.

The white sedan glided noiselessly past a father on a scooter with two children wearing school uniforms riding pillion. Traffic was slowly building up to its rush hour peak. With a beacon light on the roof of the car, it drove past traffic lights whether it was red, yellow, or green. *Maybe all that you need to get ahead in this country is a beacon vehicle...*mused the professor.

"Narayan...may I ask you something?" Rathore's voice echoed in the silent interiors of the sedan.

"Sure."

"Back in your office, I noticed every other book in your book shelf was on history except *The Art of War*. Any particular reason why?"

Narayan answered in a low tone, "That book was given to me by my father, as a birthday gift when I turned eighteen. He said this will be the only book you will ever need."

The vehicle took a left turn and entered a cobbled street. Tall trees, naked in their winter splendour, lined up straight on either side of the street. Narayan heard soft sounds of the tires navigating the intermittent nature of the cobbled street. Brake lights flashed red as the car parked near a two-storey building.

The professor stepped out of the vehicle and followed the two officers. On the outside, the building looked like any other modern day concrete monolith: faded white paint designed with bird droppings, punctuated by windowsills.

A metallic door parted open; Major Rathore had just keyed in the password. The professor was impressed and gently surprised. This is not what he had expected of the Defence Intelligence Agency when he entered the building. He assumed it would be like any ordinary government office: with ceiling fans, towering paper files, archaic chairs and tables, and yawning, lazy personnel. What he saw was a clean, wide office space with air-conditioning vents lining up the ceiling which was embedded with soft lights, and, no paper files. Computer screens were arranged with desks in a hexagonal geometric pattern. Light emitting from screens bathed the room in a soft blue halo.

Two conference cabins were placed on either side of the room lending symmetrical balance to it. Narayan was led by the two officers to the conference cabin placed to the right of the room.

The professor took his seat in a plush cushioned chair.

"She's here...good...bring her up to the conference room," Captain Veer disconnected the call and took a seat next to

Narayan. The professor folded his hands and kept it on the table.

Silence, once again, rang clear as the three men waited in the conference cabin.

And it was in this silence that the sound of anklets rushed across the room and dropped gently into the ears of the three waiting men. From the corner of his eyes, Narayan caught the graceful figure of a young woman waltzing across the room towards them. She looked jaded, tired, and exhausted but there was still an air of sophistication and elegance about her. What immediately caught the professor's eye were the sharp features of her face: a pointed nose stretching and stopping immediately beneath a set of emerald green eyes, a dimpled chin adding gravitas and sensibility to an oval jaw line. She seemed to breathe colour and life in an otherwise black and grey colour palette of the DIA.

The door of the conference cabin swung open. Her eyes slightly lowered, she entered the room. Major Rathore stood up immediately and gently extended his right hand, "Saima Azmi...?" The woman nodded her head and shook the officer's hand in a firm, confident manner. Narayan was impressed with what he saw. Very few women he knew shook hands with conviction; there was always a certain mix of hesitancy and gentleness.

"Miss Azmi..."

"Please call me Saima."

"Okay, Saima please have a seat," Major Rathore welcomed the new member.

Saima took her seat facing the professor and Captain Veer.

"Saima...the DIA would like to extend its sincere gratitude to you. The object that you have retrieved...," Captain Veer's voice tapered off.

"Is of immense value," Major Rathore concluded the line of thought.

The tired face of Saima flashed a weak smile.

"How did you manage to get your hands on Object No. 27?" Veer asked with enthusiasm.

"Maybe the lady could have some refreshments before she tells us her story," Narayan sounded out his opinion.

Captain Veer flashed a stern look at the professor.

"Good idea! I think we all could do with some coffee and breakfast," Major Rathore pressed the grey button of an intercom on the table.

"Meanwhile, could you begin with what happened yesterday?" Captain Veer looked at Saima.

This man will just not let it go, Narayan thought.

Saima collected her thoughts, took in a deep breath, "I was in the Purana Qila Museum yesterday afternoon. After a while, I noticed that Object No. 27 was missing from its case. I followed the person who took it; snatched it back from his hotel room and went to the police. That's about it."

Saima breathed in again and looked at Captain Veer.

For the second time that day, Narayan could not help but smile: a smile born out of amazement. He had half expected the woman to rattle on like an obedient child, but she had provided bullet points where the officers were looking for an informative essay. Saima had a strange effect on the professor; something that he had never experienced before.

After Saima spoke, it seemed even the room was entranced by her. Nothing moved; nobody spoke. The two officers merely looked at each other wondering what to do next.

A bell rang in the room. An attendant had brought coffee and morning refreshments. Black, steaming coffee was poured from a stainless steel vacuum flask into four, neatly arranged, white mugs. Crisply cut brown-bread sandwiches with diced vegetables in creamy mayonnaise accompanied the coffee in circular ceramic saucers.

Sips of coffee provided the energy to Captain Veer to speak again. "Saima, we would like to know a few more details of what happened yesterday."

"Sure, what do you want to know?" she replied earnestly.

"Mmm...This coffee is simply amazing. I wouldn't mind working here if I get to drink this heavenly stuff every morning," Narayan interrupted taking careful sips of his coffee.

Captain Veer was about to say something fierce to Narayan when Major Rathore jumped in, "So, Saima...at what time did you notice that the object was missing?"

"Well...it was around 3:30-ish. I was writing down something. I had observed Object No. 27 just a few minutes ago."

"Did you alert the guards?"

Saima thought for a while. "Now that you mention the guards, it was a tad strange that there were no security personnel around. As soon as I saw that it was missing from the case, I ran out of the museum hoping to catch the person who took it. And I got lucky," Saima rested her elbows on the chair.

"And how did that happen?" Major Rathore pressed on.

She took a generous sip of coffee and continued, "I saw someone leave in a black sedan just as I exited the museum. Object No. 27 was placed in the rear passenger seat of the vehicle. I could barely make it out."

"Good. Go on...," chimed Captain Veer.

"I took my scooty and followed the sedan. The pursuit led me to a lodge in a narrow street, I think, somewhere in the vicinity of Canning Road."

"You mean Madhavrao Scindia Marg?" Captain Veer pointed out.

Saima had a puzzled look on her face.

"Never mind, continue," the Captain exhaled. He wondered why people referred to the names of roads and landmarks by their British names and not their updated local identities. The post-colonial hangover was evident in the new millennium as well.

"The lodge seemed like an old fashioned resting house built by the British. It was unique; it had an antiquated feel about it, as if time had stopped functioning there," Saima took a large bite out of the sandwich and neatly wiped the residue from her lips with her index finger. She chewed on it and swallowed, followed by a sip of coffee.

Captain Veer impatiently tapped his feet on the carpeted floor.

"I walked straight to the reception. A gentle old man enquired the purpose of my visit. I fibbed that I had come to meet my uncle who had arrived in the black sedan. He kindly gave me the room number and directions. I could not believe my luck," Saima flashed a gorgeous smile.

"The room was still and absolutely silent. Crouched near the door, I thought for an instant whether the old man had pulled my leg and given me the wrong room number. A voice talking over the phone about the object quelled my doubts. After a few seconds, the voice trailed off. I could make out that the man had entered the washroom and had run a bath. With a few twists and turns of my hairpin, I managed to unlock the door after a few attempts. Something I learned from my father as a kid."

Major Rathore's eyebrows shot up in surprise.

Narayan's attention had caught a slight twitch of her left ear as Saima narrated her story. The visual tick appeared when she narrated her experience. It had happened a couple of times now.

"I entered the room and tiptoed inside in the quietest way possible. The bath was still running," Saima spoke animatedly with her hands moving in sharp angles. "The object was nowhere in sight. I had to make a quick decision: whether to leave or to stick around and search for the object. I ran my eyes all over the room. And then I saw it. The emerald green halo emanating from a half closed cupboard."

"It all seems very convenient," Captain Veer questioned Saima.

She ignored the enquiry and continued, "I picked out the object when a heavy hand held my shoulder," Saima paused, collecting herself, "The next few moments went by in a blur. The hand held my shoulder and flung me to a corner of the room. I crashed into a wall but held on to the object. A well built man with grey hair advanced towards me. He was about to grab me when I summoned all my strength and swung my arms, while holding the object, at his torso. The man buckled with the impact of the object hitting his torso, but recovered soon enough to land a blow on my back as I tried to escape."

Saima paused once again. It seemed as if she was fighting back her tears and sniffed.

"Please have a glass of water," Major Rathore offered.

Her slender fingers grabbed a clear glass of water; her throat bobbed up and down, gulping the water.

"I got up using my elbow and the support of the dressing table. My eyes fell on a paperweight. I grabbed it without thinking and threw it in the direction of that beast..."

Anger seems to add an aura of beauty to her, Narayan mused, his attention focused gently on Saima.

"He screamed and I ran..."

The professor could only manage to pay attention to the conclusion of that sentence, missing the link in between.

Tears trickled down Saima Azmi's marble-white cheeks. She quickly wiped it the same way she had wiped off the sandwich residue from her lips – in a clinical manner.

"Does it sound convenient now officer?" Saima shot a look at Captain Veer, who turned to look at his partner.

"Saima, would you like to rest for a while?" the gentle voice of Major Rathore enquired. "We understand you have had a long night. The DIA has a comfortable guest room where you can run a warm bath and catch your forty winks," a naughty smile broke across the officer's face as he continued. "Veer likes to laze off and often sleeps in the guest room...even when he is on duty."

"What the...," Captain Veer looked at his partner wondering where this came from.

"It is absolutely true. I have the clip on my phone. And the way he snores...it is a miracle his wife still puts up with him," winked Major Rathore.

Captain Veer silently sipped his coffee.

Saima's lips parted to reveal a smile. She pulled open the zip of her shoulder bag in a straight line. Narayan observed the diamond imprint on her bag.

A green hexagonal object emerged from the black bag held by white, elongated fingers. The fingers trembled ever so slightly as if it knew and understood the weight of history it was carrying.

Saima placed Object. No 27 on the sky blue laminate table.

Once again, the elastic quality of time allowed it to slow down, almost to a stop.

Narayan made the first move, jolting awake the sense of time of the two officers in the room. He leaned forward and laid his hands on the emerald-green object, running through it, as if memorizing each and every detail. The magnificence of the object, reflected in Narayan's eyes, could not even begin to compare with the image that was shown to him earlier.

"Jaaa keh men der newr setarh ha bh 'enewan khewanedh shedh…A place where I read in the light of stars," the professor's voice echoed across the cabin, attaching to it a sense of prophecy.

"That is amazing…I did not even know there was script embedded on the object. Have you learnt Farsi before?" asked Saima, her graceful body leaning ever so slightly towards the professor.

"Thank you, Saima." Captain Veer interrupted the professor curtly, "This is a very important break for us. Now, if you would like to retire to our guest room…," Captain Veer tapped on his wristwatch looking at Narayan to indicate they were on the clock.

"Thanks…," Saima got up from her chair. Major Rathore buzzed for an attendant. "The attendant will lead you to our guest room."

The sound of anklets faded into the background.

"I do not believe her. There is something that does not add up," Captain Veer voiced his concern.

"What's not to believe? She just handed over the missing object," countered Narayan.

"What Veer is trying to say is that we need to be sure that she is telling the truth," Major Rathore defended his partner. "Have you been able to figure out what the script on the object refers to?"

"Yes, pretty much," answered Narayan to the Major's query. "How good is your history?"

"Not good enough, I'm afraid," replied the Major. "Why do you ask?"

"Let me start from the beginning then…"

"How long is this going to take now?" Captain Veer interjected.

Narayan looked at Major Rathore. "Continue," replied the Major.

"But Sir…"

"Continue Narayan, I'm all ears."

"Okay," Narayan's body straightened with attention, "Babur was the first Mughal emperor. Humayun, his son, inherited the throne and became the Mughal dynasty's second emperor. This," the professor pointed to Object No. 27, "belonged to Humayun. 'A place where I read in the light of stars'…The emperor loved to watch the stars at night and considered himself an avid astronomer; hence the script in Farsi. One of the towers in Purana Qila, built by Babur, was a library with the top floor serving as a reading room and a gazing deck. Humayun would spend hours reading the stars," Narayan's index finger pointed up, "and perusing literature, poetry," the professor's finger traced a line down to the laminate table.

"A connecting line between heaven and earth," mulled Major Rathore.

"That's an interesting thought," reflected Narayan.

Captain Veer continued to tap his feet on the ground impatiently, waiting for the history lesson to end.

"It is ironical that this library Humayun loved to spend time in became the backdrop of his death."

"How did that happen," Major Rathore's interest piqued.

"Do we have the time for it?" Narayan glanced at Captain Veer.

"Please continue professor," Major Rathore requested.

"Very well then. The emperor had a habit of offering namaz whenever he heard the call to prayer. It could be anywhere – battlefield, royal garden, bath – Humayun kneeled down and paid his obeisance to the Almighty. In my opinion, it was his way of reinforcing a belief that this material world is just a temporary illusion."

The Major listened in rapt attention.

"One evening as Humayun climbed down a flight of stairs of his library with a couple of books in hand, he heard the call to prayer. As was his habit, he kneeled down. While kneeling down, his robe entwined around his feet, causing him to trip and fall down the flight of stairs," Narayan paused. "The fall killed him."

"Rather unfortunate," commented Major Rathore.

"You must be careful of what you love; it could kill you," smirked Captain Veer.

Narayan caught the figure of Saima from the corner of his eye walking across the glass facade of the conference cabin.

"This object is a symbol of Humayun's love for astronomy and was probably kept in his library," concluded the professor.

A gentle knock on the cabin door alerted the attention of Major Rathore. He gestured Saima to enter the cabin. The door opened.

"I have a request."

Major Rathore got a good look at Saima for the first time, "Proceed..."

Saima entered the room, closely followed by her rustling anklets and took her seat. "I would like to know why there is a clamour for this object. What is it that the DIA and the brute that attacked me, are chasing after?"

"Miss Azmi," Captain Veer spoke authoritatively, "We thank you for your valuable assistance. Rest assured, you will be rewarded for your efforts. The situation we have on our hands is sensitive and the information is privy to a few. It would be best if you let us take it from here."

"Okay, I will do that. But answer this question: who will ensure my protection?" Saima flashed her eyes at the officer, "Since the assailant has already seen my face from close quarters and can identify me, I would like to know who would protect me from another attack."

The officers looked at each other.

"I don't think I can trust my life in the hands of the local police force. I would rather be a part of this team," Saima pointed to the three men in the room, "Or whatever it is you are planning."

"Listen lady...," Captain Veer voice gathered steam.

"Veer...," came the calm reminder from his partner. Captain Veer took a deep breath and exhaled. Major Rathore shifted his gaze to Saima, "Let us play it by ear. For now you are welcome to be a part of this room, that is, if history does not bore you."

Saima flashed an appreciative smile.

"This just keeps getting better and better," murmured Captain Veer under his breath.

"I have given my history lesson. Gentlemen, if you have no further use of me, I would like to take your leave."

"Hold on, Narayan," Major Rathore requested.

Captain Veer took over, "One thing we have not been able to establish is whether the person we spotted yesterday," the Captain deliberately concealed the name of Major Salim Khan, "and this object in our possession have a concrete link. Was he behind the theft of Object No. 27 from the museum? His presence at the museum clearly points to a link."

"Who is the..."

"Narayan," Captain Veer cut Saima's enquiry mid-sentence, "Tell us if you can think of why the person would want this object."

Narayan's mind tried to draw a parallel. It ran through the various threads of history and politics, trying to connect the two. A couple of minutes passed. Narayan was silent.

"Let us visit this library of Humayun in Purana Qila. Maybe we could find a lead there," Major Rathore offered a way ahead.

"Why not the museum where the object was stolen from?" enquired Captain Veer.

"We can visit the museum after we've examined the library," replied Major Rathore.

"Isn't Humayun's library off access to the general public?"

"But we are not the general public, professor," Major smiled. "Veer, inform the ASI (Archaeological Survey of India) authorities. Professor Shastri, since your students are very important to you, please inform them that you will be with us for the remainder of the day."

Narayan flashed a wry smile, "Let's move."

5

Saima placed her feet on the ground and alighted gently from the sedan. An immediate "Wow," escaped Saima, as she looked at the historical edifice in front of her: Sher Mandal. Her deep, brown eyes rested on the octagonal shape of the structure, taking in intricacies of the architecture: large, red sandstone bricks that weaved around the two-storied tower, horseshoe-shaped archways imprinted with white stars, and a stray bird or two nestled in a corner.

The early morning had transformed into a clear day, with mild sunshine streaming beams of light through trees, casting soft shadows on the manicured lawn surrounding Sher Mandal. Sweepers swept away brown autumn leaves from the base of trees in swift strokes, using long-reach aluminium rakes.

"Saima..."

Her attention came back to the present moment; Major Rathore gestured to follow them into Sher Mandal.

The officer led the way followed by Captain Veer and Narayan. Saima followed behind soaking in a sense of culture and timeless history.

A couple of officials from ASI stood at attention near the entrance. Major Rathore nodded to the two officials and entered. A central dome arched high, detailed with colourful ceramic wall art, imposed its presence over the visitors, and provided a gateway into the past.

Narayan craned his neck up to catch the detailing of the dome. In a way, these walls carry a record of our nation. Things that have happened, are happening, will happen in the future, imprinted on these bricks...thought Narayan.

"Though this tower was Humayun's library, it is called Sher Mandal after Sher Shah Suri, who captured Purana Qila when Humayun went away on an expedition and ruled for five years," Narayan's voice echoed across the empty stairwell as the group of four climbed the steep stairs of the tower.

"Thank you Narayan," Major Rathore spoke between breaths, "If only I had known you during my school days, I would have aced my history test, not flunked it,"The Major tried to inject a bit of dry humour.

Soles of shoes slapped gently on the steps, and stepped up.

A large, wide room came into view. Windows punctuated the circumference of the room allowing its residents a panoramic view of the surroundings. The protective glass attached itself to the open windows, offering the library a sense of protection from the elements, even time itself. For a reading room that was centuries old, it was well preserved offering a glimpse of a dynasty that shaped the cultural and geographical perspective of the Indian Subcontinent.

Captain Veer carried Object No. 27 into the room and placed it carefully on a makeshift table, in the centre of the room. The emerald green object transformed from an inanimate piece of antiquity to Sher Mandal's nerve centre: every action and every word spoken would be about the artefact.

Rows of shelves lined portions of the room. The passage of centuries reflected clearly on the inhabitants of the shelves: manuscripts and books. Pages of the manuscript had turned dusty brown with its Persian and Arabic script faded at the edges. Hard covers of the books were spongy to touch, flaking at its borders.

The shallow dome ceiling of the room was a mute spectator to the proceedings below: Major Avinash Singh Rathore, like a lead conductor, orchestrated the piece – pointing his invisible baton to the professor and Saima who turned their attention to the books and manuscripts, pointing his invisible baton to Captain Veer who began to examine every nook and corner. The movement – of characters to and from the shelves, around the room, in and out of the room, pages of books delicately opened, manuscripts rolled out patiently, attendants carrying flasks and casseroles, steam escaping from a flask flipped open, morsels of white rice and yellow dal curry disappearing from plates – morphed into one another representing a visual ballet played to the beat of ticking time.

The sun had traced its path and now kissed the horizon with its orange glow. Saima closed her eyes, standing near a window, basking in the warmth of the setting sun. Narayan ran his eyes across the shelves once again, in case he missed something. Major Rathore gazed at an empty wall, reflective of his state of mind. Captain Veer paced around the room, restlessness a part of his personality.

Object No. 27 sat on the table, perfectly still, just as it had in the morning.

"I think we are done here," Narayan's voice served as a curtain call to the ballet.

Saima shot a glance at the professor.

"Sher Mandal seems like a dead end. Books and manuscripts hold no clue; did the gentlemen have any luck?" the professor adjusted his spectacles.

Major Rathore shook his head. Captain Veer walked out of the room: his face tense, fists closed, taking long strides. The echo of his footsteps faded quickly.

The professor looked at the Major in an enquiring manner. "Veer's just a little frustrated," replied Major, "he takes his work a little too seriously at times…but you are right. I think it is time we called it a day."

Captain Veer stood on the manicured lawn outside the edifice. Droplets of dew on the crew-cut grass soaked the outer sole of the officer's shoe, giving it a darker shade of black than its body. The sky too wore different shades: dark orange washed the hemisphere with azure blue fading into its lighter shade. Captain Veer noticed a lone bird in the sky, silhouetted against the setting sky. Yellow flickered on the wings of the bird gliding from one tip to the other. It looked like the bird was surfing the rays of the sunset.

A hand placed itself on Captain Veer's left shoulder. The officer turned.

"Everything all right?" Major Rathore enquired.

Veer forced a smile.

Saima and Narayan walked towards the two officers.

"Narayan, is that you?"

Narayan stopped in his stride and adjusted the frames of his spectacles; his eyes brought to focus a thin, tall man, drooping slightly at the shoulders with greying hair portioned at the centre of his forehead. An ASI badge was fixed on his shirt pocket. Saima stopped a few feet away from the professor.

"Ramesh Uncle?" Narayan's voice had a hint of suspicion.

"Yes, my boy. Ramesh Moorthy. You do recognize me," the man walked to Narayan and shook his hand.

"How did you know it was me?" Narayan's eyes flashed genuine surprise. "The last time I saw you, I think, I was still wearing shorts."

"I always knew that you would grow up to be a tall handsome fellow," Ramesh Moorthy smiled. "Besides, when the DIA contacted our office today morning with their request, I guessed the history professor in the team might be Mrs. Shastri's son," Ramesh Moorthy kept his right hand on Narayan's right shoulder.

"I read in the papers a couple of years ago that a paper you published got rave reviews. Well done, I am happy for you."

"Thanks."

"How is your father doing?"

Narayan was silent.

"Looks like I asked the wrong question...," Moorthy's voice trailed.

Saima sensed the professor's discomfort when his father was mentioned.

"Narayan...the memories of you tagging along with your mother on her archaeological surveys is like it happened just yesterday. Do you remember?"

Narayan nodded and smiled.

"I would always have a bar of chocolate in hand for you. Chocolate uncle is what you would call me."

The ageing ASI officer produced a bar of chocolate covered in blue wrapping, "This one's for you," he offered Narayan.

Saima smiled at this heart warming gesture.

"Thanks uncle, it is very kind of you," Narayan took the chocolate and slid it into his pocket.

"No thanks needed. I'm just happy to see you all grown up and doing extremely well for yourself. I' m not surprised, though. You were a bright kid with a curious mind. I remember this one time you asked your mother, 'if the sun and moon can cast shadows, why can't stars?' Your mother did not have an answer."

Narayan's mind latched on to *why stars can't cast shadows*. The rest of what the ASI officer said was muted from the professor's ears.

"If you need..."

"Uncle...you are a godsend," the professor hugged Ramesh Moorthy and began to run towards Sher Mandal.

"Nara..." Ramesh Moorthy was taken aback.

Major Rathore and Captain Veer saw the professor run through the lawn like a champion sprinter. The two officers set their bodies in motion as well.

It took a second for Saima to comprehend what was going on. Her graceful figure too began to head for the two-storied tower.

Narayan's feet barely landed on the steps as his body flew across the flight of stairs.

"Looks like the professor is on some kind of steroids...," commented Captain Veer to his partner as the two officer tried to catch up.

Narayan burst into the library and quickly made his way to a window. The professor stopped, with his hands on his knees, and took deep, relaxing breaths.

A muezzin's sonorous call for prayers filtered through the window. Stars grew brighter in the twilight sky.

The two DIA officers burst into the room and came to a stop. A couple of minutes later, Saima entered the room.

Narayan looked across the room. His eyes scanned every nook and corner. And then it came to sight: the faintest of shadows shimmied around a corner. The shadow was so faint that it seemed like an inhabitant of the room rather than an evening guest. Narayan walked to the corner and lunged down on his knees. A miniature white star was traced on the red sandstone brick. He traced an imaginary path from the white star to the brightest star in the sky, the pole star. Narayan felt that the pole star was casting the almost imperceptible shadow on its mirror figure.

"Narayan," the Major called out and the professor immediately held up his hand, requesting Major for silence. Captain Veer looked at his partner.

Narayan observed a triangle-shaped dent on the sandstone brick next to the image of the white star. He placed his right hand on the brick and tried to push it. The brick did not budge.

"Something fits in here, a triangle shaped object."

Saima's eyes landed on Object No. 27. She picked it up from the table and handed it over to Shastri.

"Eureka," the professor flashed a wide smile to Saima. He quickly placed the stone on the brick and gently pushed it. The brick moved in slightly, releasing a puff of white dust.

Major Rathore and Captain Veer looked on in surprise as a portion of the shelf, to their right, creaked open.

Narayan got up and leaned against the opening. The square frame of his spectacle peered into darkness, "We need light."

Saima zipped open a bag and brought forth a flashlight. The two officers took a few steps closer to Narayan and Saima.

White light rushed into the darkness, as Saima switched on the flashlight, and struck, what looked like, two manuscript scrolls.

"Gentlemen...Saima...we have our clue," beamed the professor, flashing the look of a jackpot winner.

Two scrolls of paper breathed, for the first time, the new millennium air.

"We need to be careful," Narayan took a few steps back and made his way to a black box placed on the ground some feet away. The black box looked like a suitcase. Narayan gently flipped open the top on its hinges. The box was divided into compartments carrying packets of sanitized gloves, thin plastic forceps, and transparent plastic laminations: items which belonged to the Archaeological Survey of India, used for conserving and preserving ancient manuscripts.

The professor tore open a fresh packet of white gloves, slipped it on his hands, and then took a pair of plastic forceps along with two plastic laminates.

Saima continued to shine the flashlight on the manuscripts. Narayan crouched at the opening and stretched his hands towards the manuscripts. He nudged one manuscript into the plastic laminate with the forceps, then repeated the same careful sequence of steps with the second manuscript.

Two ancient manuscripts lay on the table sealed in present day plastic laminates.

The eyes of Narayan, Saima and the two officers peered at the first manuscript.

A candle burns bright, the flame sharp and pointed, in the still room. It casts its yellow halo on a fair face lined with black facial hair. Bristles of a navy blue feather slant slightly outward with its sharpened white tip poised over a blank sheet of paper. A drop of black ink coated the tip, but it seemed frozen, like the hand holding the quill.

The quill is placed gently on the dark brown desk. The flame of the candle flickers for an instant. A man gets up from the desk and walks towards the window of his spacious room. Books are lined across shelves accompanying the walls of the room. Dressed in a saffron robe lined with blue prints at its edges, the man rests his palms on the windowsill and leans outside. A cool night breeze wafts across the figure, rustling the robe. The man looks at the sky where a full moon sits with is consort of twinkling stars. The night is bathed in white light streaming from the diamond in the sky. A surge of emotions fills the silhouetted figure, but he does not know how to articulate them.

He turns away from the window, and walks back to his desk. The tip of the quill is refreshed with black ink; the wrist begins to guide the quill across the sheet of paper. Words begin to form on it:

I do not know whether I should articulate my feelings on this letter as an emperor addressing a future heir, or as a father would talk to his son. I hope my heart can guide my hand in this endeavour.

Summer is giving way to autumn. I believe that our empire, of which you will be the ruler one day, too will have its peak and its natural ebb, like the seasons. You will be the glorious sun that shines on our dynasty, my son.

I may not have been by your side as you grew. My thoughts, however, were always focused on your progress and well being. Many a night as I lay in bed after a hard day's battle, not knowing what tomorrow will bring, I drew strength from the hope that I will see you when I return home.

There was a time when we lost everything, when we wandered distant lands as nomads without a place to call home. Having regained our kingdom, our legacy will now continue through your deeds. Jalal[1], my son, you will have to be a gentle shepherd who guides his flock, be like a steady rock amidst the flowing river stream. People will look to you for guidance and deliverance, for love and peace, but most importantly, for fairness and justice. Do not be bound by religious dogma, instead appreciate and respect the sentiments of your non-Muslim brothers and sisters. Whenever you are in doubt, trust your heart and hear the voice of your soul. It will never mislead you because it will always reveal the message of the almighty – our saviour and protector.

The land that touches your feet is glorious. Your Abba Huzuur[2] once told me an anecdote that served as an internal illumination to his soul. This incident happened shortly after he had conquered the Agra fort. It was early morning and your Abba Huzuur was taking in the sights of a sunrise on a cold winter morning from the terrace of the fort dressed in a woollen robe. A man bathing in the cold stream of the Yamuna, which ran along the periphery of the fort, caught his eye. He became curious and decided to meet the man.

Your Abba Huzuur shouted to the man from the banks of the stream, enquiring how he could take a bath in the open on such a cold morning. The man replied that he had faith in his god, Bholenath, and it was this faith that kept him warm. Having just conquered the fort, your Abba Huzzur tried to display his pride and told the man that he was now the man's master and lord, and that the man's life was in his hands now. The Brahmin replied with a smile that his life would always be in the hands of

---

[1] Akbar

[2] Babur

Bholenath and not some wandering looter who would take our wealth back to where he came from.

Abba Huzuur did not know what to say. He stood silent. He turned back quietly and walked away. Can you imagine a man, who had just won a bloody battle did not have the stomach to reply to the bathing man who was unarmed and only half clothed. What the Brahmin had told him echoed in his conscience.

Later that day, when he went hunting, he was gravely wounded by a leopard[3]. As he lay, resting his back on the bark of a tree, a Sufi saint crossing the forest gave him the elixir of life – water. Abba Huzuur always carried a large diamond with him, which he had found in Badalgarh fort. The stone was offered to the saint as reward. Smiling, the saint refused to take the stone saying that this rock was a gift from Allah the Almighty, and would be a lucky omen for you and your future lineage as well. He should ensure that it passed from one generation to the next.

When the saint left, your Abba Huzuur had an epiphany. He decided to adopt this land as his own to give rise to a dynasty, founded by him, that would be remembered forever. A dynasty that would be remembered not for its thievery and brutality, but for its enlightenment and fair rule of the land.

The diamond has since passed on from him to me, and now from me to you. Remember, as long as you have that blessing from the Almighty Allah, no harm will come to you.

Bigger and brighter than the two Noors[4], unlocked by the 'Key of Fortune', the fortune of the Mughal Dynasty.

---

[3] Prologue

[4] Koh-i-Noor, Darya-ye Noor

In my heart, I know that your name will ring the loudest when our dynasty is recalled in the future.

I hope these words have expressed to you the depth of my emotions.

Allah hafij, Jalal. My love will always be with you…

The hand withdraws the quill from the sheet of paper and rests on the desk, light and peaceful.

"I hope these words have expressed to you the depth of my emotions. Allah hafij, Jalal. My love will always be with you…," the low voice of Narayan made it audible for the audience of three in the library of Sher Mandal. The eyes and ears of Major Rathore, Captain Veer and Saima were locked in on Narayan, hanging on to every word, every audible sound.

The manuscript scroll in the sealed laminate was light brown in colour with a majestic royal blue emblem – a hemisphere dotted with white stars etched on the header of the scroll. Square golden lines framed the scroll like a portrait, with letters of Farsi etched within it in thin calligraphic strokes. The scroll was centuries old, and revealed it in its faded scripts, and delicately deteriorating paper.

Narayan's gaze shifted to the second manuscript: it was shorter in comparison to the first. Faint moonlight streamed in through the windows and rested on the manuscripts providing an ephemeral glow. The second manuscript was without pomp and gaiety – calligraphic letters of Farsi scripted in black ink on faded brown sheet of paper. Narayan Shastri's eyes scanned the entire scroll in a matter of seconds.

"This is another letter, albeit an appeal, from Humayun to his trusted general, Bairam Khan. The emperor requests his general to guide his son in the matters of state and military strategies in Humayun's absence," the professor relaxed his eyes.

The chirp of nocturnal insects rose to a slow crescendo as the group of four tried to assimilate the information that had just been revealed.

"If the two scrolls are here, is it possible that the letters were never delivered to their intended recipients?" Captain Veer enquired.

"Just like we have copies and backups today, the Mughals too had their version of a copy. An important letter, document, or proclamation would be written out twice: one serving as the original, and the second, a copy. These letters that I am holding are, in fact, copies of the original letters. Quite intelligent, don't you think," replied Narayan.

"How can you say for sure?" Saima asked the professor.

"This emblem," Shastri pointed to the blue seal in the header, "would contain golden stars if it were the original."

"That…is simply brilliant," Major Rathore was truly impressed by the depth of Narayan's expertise.

Captain Veer too nodded his head, agreeing with his partner. Saima had a soft smile playing on her lips.

"Narayan, is it the Koh-i-Noor Humayun is referring to as the 'fortune of the Mughals' in his letter?"

Narayan brought his left hand to the frames of his spectacles and adjusted it slightly. It was a behavioural tick which helped Narayan to clear his mind. His eyes focused gently on the windows of the room.

"It is neither Koh-i-Noor that Humayun is referring to, nor is it the Darya-ye Noor."

"Darya-ye Noor?"

"One of the biggest diamonds in the world, the Darya-ye Noor is considered to be the 'double' of Koh-i-Noor," replied Narayan to Major Rathore's query.

"It says in this letter, that this sacred diamond was bigger than Koh-i-Noor and its double. Hmm...," Narayan deliberated rubbing his chin.

Object No. 27, placed back on the table after unlocking the secret door, sat still, soaking in the night.

"Maybe it is that mystery diamond whose existence has long been debated," Narayan looked at the three. A look of excitement crossed his face, "There is this unnamed Hindu king of Gwalior, whose name has been lost in the pages of history, who had three prized diamonds in his treasury: the two Noors and this mystery diamond. The king donated the three stones to the Man Kameshwar Mahadev temple in Agra. Eyes of the Shiva idol in the temple were the two Noors while the third stone was the Lord's third eye and sat on the forehead, becoming the idol's centrepiece. "

Major Rathore caught Saima fiddling with her phone from the corner of his eye.

"This mystery diamond," Narayan continued, "was three times larger than its famous cousin, the Kohinoor, and the stone's worth is believed to be equivalent to an amount that could feed the entire world for two-and-a-half days."

"Interesting...," remarked Captain Veer, "anything more to this mystery diamond?"

"This stone has been mentioned in the *Baburnama*, Babur's memoir. The king of Gwalior had to yield his treasured possession to 'Alauddn Khilji in 1294. The three stones travelled from the courts of the Tughlaq dynasty to the Lodi dynasty before Babur seized it from Ibrahim Lodi," Narayan looked at the two manuscripts.

"Hmm...what about the 'key of fortune' that is mentioned in the letter? Does it refer to the mystery diamond?"

Narayan took a couple of steps and walked towards the window. Peering out of the window, the professor took a deep breath. His mind was in overdrive connecting the various threads that had been found in this room. "Probably not," he replied turning to Major Rathore, "The 'key of fortune' clearly alludes to a key that would unlock a safe of some sort which is holding the mystery diamond." Narayan walked back to the group.

Captain Veer's eyes focused on the manuscript, "If it is not the diamond, then what could be the 'Key of Fortune'?" the Captain wondered aloud.

Narayan was silent. No clue appeared in his mind.

"Professor, may I take a closer look at the letter?" Saima's request seemed like a welcome break. Narayan looked at Major Rathore, the Major nodded in the affirmative.

Thin, slender fingers of Saima ran lightly across the firm surface of the laminate. Her eyes moved left to right, eyelashes dancing to its own tune, as she read the entire letter. The fingers lifted off the laminate, Saima's visage cracked a smile.

"The key of fortune," Saima spoke slowly drumming up the tension, "is in our very midst."

This response was met with three pairs of surprised eyebrows.

"Gentlemen, it is often said that a man's fortune lies in his stars…," Saima paced her words carefully.

Narayan's eyes lit up. He had figured it out. He half opened his mouth to reveal the answer but shut it. He didn't want to steal Saima's spotlight.

Saima took a couple of steps, gracefully, to Object No. 27. The two officers looked at her, carefully measuring her every move. "A place where I read in the light of stars… Stars are linked to 'fortune'…," she picked up the emerald green stone.

"Of course…Object No. 27 is the 'key of fortune'," Captain Veer announced bringing an end to the round of trivia.

The room and its four occupants were now bathed in the diffused glow of a winter moon. There was no source of external or artificial light to illuminate the room. In their excitement, no one had bothered about it as well.

"That was an incredible display of deduction, Saima, simply superb," Narayan acknowledged.

"Glad I could contribute," Saima replied with a hint of modesty. She placed the object back on the table.

"Okay, we have the key. Now all we have to do is find its lock," Captain Veer chirped followed by the crescendo of crickets which took centre stage.

Minutes ticked away. The room fell silent once again. Each individual was lost in his or her train of thought. Three things raced through Major Rathore's thoughts: the mystery diamond, Major Salim Khan, and the visit of an ex US President to Taj Mahal. No line seemed to connect the three dots. "I think it's time we called it a day," the officer said looking at his partner, "I can barely see your face, Veer."

Soft laughter broke across the room.

"We have had a good day today. Let's continue tomorrow. Veer, tell the officials to pack Object No. 27, the scrolls, and deliver it to headquarters tonight. Professor, Saima, after you," Major Rathore pointed his hand towards the exit.

6

A white sedan carrying Narayan and Saima coursed through the hazy, winter night. Tiny dots of transparent mist had formed on the windows of the car. Trying to count the number of dots, Saima mused whether this was how a fish inside an aquarium felt, covered with drops of water.

The city of New Delhi was covered in a blanket of yellow glow beaming from streetlights. Yellow seemed to be the motif of the night: people huddled around flames of yellow, jumping up from sticks of wood and autumn leaves, to keep their hands warm in the cold; steaming hot yellow pakwans served straight from deep frying pans to customers relishing it with bowls of yellow dal; succulent pieces of meat dipped in turmeric paste cooked over open charcoal grills.

Colours and hues of the night stood in stark contrast to that of the day.

Streetlights lining the roads were soon replaced by rows of peepal trees hanging on to their last shred of autumn leaves. The sedan had turned left into a private driveway, leading straight to a wrought iron gate. Lights of the vehicle shone on the curved lines embedded on the gate, bringing a guard clothed in multiple layers of woollen sweaters and a jacket, with a thick brown shawl wrapped around his head.

The gate opened slowly, the creak of its hinges announcing the act to the night.

The sedan crept inside the gate and stopped after a couple of yards. A two-storied mansion towered the car. The guard ambled quickly to the car and opened the rear passenger door.

"This is where you live?" Saima asked the professor, her eyes reflecting surprise.

Earlier, at Sher Mandal, Saima had put forth a request that she would like to stay with Narayan, if he did not object to it. Captain Veer was apprehensive about the idea. Saima reasoned that the professor's house would be the last place her assailant would look for her. Narayan went with the idea; he was looking forward to the prospect of getting to know the woman who had impressed him with her dignity and intelligence. Major Rathore had called in a second sedan to take Narayan and Saima to their desired location.

Captain Veer and Major Rathore cruised through the streets.

"Swati will be happy to see you home early."

"I hope so," replied Captain Veer to his partner shooting a quick look at his watch: the hour hand was on eight. "It will be good to be home a little early. It's just been one thing after another. First, the blasts, then the Taj Mahal visit by you know who, and now Major Salim Khan...the list is endless."

Major Rathore nodded his head, "How about kiddo? Am sure she misses you."

"Yeah, she does. Even when I spend some time with Swati and kiddo, the back of my mind is constantly ticking, thinking about work. I am not able to establish a sincere connect with them. It feels like I am watching images on a screen which I cannot touch or feel." Captain Veer shook his head.

The sedan drove in a straight line.

"How are things with you?" Captain Veer shifted his eyes from the steering wheel to Major Rathore.

"Okay. Work keeps me busy and, more importantly, distracted. I have been thinking whether Major Salim's presence has anything to do with the Taj Mahal visit," replied the officer changing tracks of the conversation.

"I have been thinking about the same thing. Hopefully the professor can help us figure it out," Captain Veer tapped his fingers on the wheel to a beat running in his head, "I have been thinking about Saima. What do..."

"Should Swati be worried?" grinned Major Rathore.

"Sir please...what do you think of her?"

"Well, she is smart, beautiful, looks like a strong character..."

"Enough with the clichés. Do you trust her?"

"I guess so. So far I have no reason not to."

"Her story still does not convince me.

Captain Veer's voice trailed. The two officers fell silent and looked ahead in the distance.

The sedan melted away in the distance in the yellow haze.

7

Saima's brown eyes stretched wide to take in the décor of the living room. A crystal chandelier hung delicately from the ceiling, bathing the room in a gentle white glow. Elaborately carved ceramic pillars stood guard over the four corners. Thick curtains, reflecting a shade of indigo, flowed over the windows, furnishing the room with an additional sense of comfort and warmth. She observed the brown, stone walls catching flickers of white light, which gave the physical space a sense of its past.

Narayan was talking on the phone, pacing around the room, taking a bite of the chocolate bar, "Uncle, I am so sorry I had to run out on you abruptly. If I hadn't reached the room in time, the clue... We shall meet soon. It was great seeing you today after a long time."

Saima overheard bits and pieces of the conversation. A servant walked into the room carrying a tray containing a pot and two cups. Having placed the tray on a stone-carved, grey centre table, the servant left the room. The faint shimmer of silver caught Saima's eye. The tray, pot, and cups were made of silver.

"Saima, would you like some coffee? It's freshly brewed filter coffee," the professor walked to the table.

"Are you a prince or some sort of royalty?" asked Saima with a half curious look knitted across her eyebrows.

"Nope," Shastri replied, "But I do get asked that question almost every time a guest comes over."

"Stone walls, ceramic pillars, chandeliers...the décor of this place screams royal ancestry. And to top that, you serve coffee in silver trays," Saima's smile lingered as she took a seat on a plush, leather sofa, which had an angular frame of a throne.

Narayan sat facing Saima. "The truth is...," he poured coffee form the pot into the two cups, "when I was studying History in college, I was the favourite student of a particular professor. He became a father figure to me, fuelling my interest and passion for Indian History. We would have long conversations, discussing various eras and dynasties. He had an interesting observation. The professor believed that dynasties that stood the test of time always had a strong woman personality working behind the scenes."

Saima took a careful sip from the steaming cup while keeping her eyes on Narayan.

"He did not have a family; so, when he passed away I was declared the owner of his mansion, this mansion, by his will."

"Wow…you are truly blessed," Saima kept her cup on the table. "What about your family?"

Narayan sipped his coffee and stared into the distance. Saima felt that she had intruded on an uncomfortable issue.

"The way you deduced that Object No. 27 was the Key of Fortune was mighty impressive," Narayan's response clearly indicated that family was something he did not want to talk about.

Saima placed her hands over the cup of coffee allowing the steam to stream through her fingers. "The thing is that I am an interior designer. A friend of mine wanted me to design the décor of her house. She has always been fascinated with the Mughal period and its style and wanted it to blend in with the living space. For the past few months, I have been reading up on the intricacies of Mughal architecture. The jali work, crescent and star motifs, gemstones. Its grandeur and opulence took my breath away."

Saima took a sip from her cup, "Yesterday, I was at the museum looking at the various relics, searching for inspiration." Narayan listened attentively in between sips of coffee. For the second time that day, he observed the slight twitch of her left ear as she spoke. "Who knew my search for inspiration would land me in a treasure hunt," Saima looked at the professor.

"Food is served," the servant's voice announced.

A delectable spread of sarson da saag and makki di roti served with a generous dollop of butter greeted Narayan and Saima. The two of them finished their meal silently and quickly, relishing the fare.

"They say that a clean plate after dinner is usually a sign of a delicious meal."

"I agree," Saima responded with a content look on her face.

"Saima, would you like to retire to your room?"

"Not right now, my mind is still buzzing with the clues and information we discovered today. I would like to delve deeper and find out about the lock of our Key."

The servant placed two fingerbowls. Shastri gave a good squeeze to the fresh lemon wedge dipping in warm water and cleansed his fingers. Saima simply dipped her fingers and wiped it dry in her napkin, the lemon wedge untouched.

Shastri looked at his dinner companion, "I am going to do some reading. Hopefully I can stumble upon a clue."

"I will join you then. Who knows, maybe I will figure it out before you do," smiled Saima.

The two figures climbed a flight of stairs which were wide and ornately carved, and made their way to a study.

The study was Spartan by design, with a wooden shelf neatly stacked with thick volumes of history, literature, and philosophy. To the right wall of the room was a mattress covered with a thick blanket. A wooden desk with an ergonomic cushion chair sat adjacent to the wall near the entrance. A square mirror, large enough to reflect the head and shoulders of the person staring at it, framed with a detailed bronze border enveloped with rust, hung to the left of the desk. The blank screen of an iPad, resting on top of the desk, reflected Narayan and Saima's visage.

"Professor…"

"Call me Narayan," the professor turned to the bookshelf with Saima standing behind him.

"Okay, Narayan, is it true that you turned down an offer to teach at Princeton?"

The question took Narayan by surprise. He adjusted the frame of his spectacles getting a better look at his house guest, "How did you know?"

"Google," Saima stated matter-of-factly. "So, it is true, then."

Narayan simply smiled and turned his attention back to his shelf.

"May I ask why?"

"Well…it was a long time ago," Narayan had a maroon-coloured hardbound tome in his hand, "I had always wanted to teach here, teach students about our glorious past, about our kings, queens, and emperors. I felt I had a role to play in India. And I am glad I stayed back," Narayan handed over the tome to Saima, "Otherwise I might not have met you."

Saima smiled and looked at the heavy volume in her hand: *Akbarnama*.

"Since the Key of Fortune was given to Akbar, the emperor should lead us to the next clue," Narayan sat on his desk and switched on the iPad. Saima made herself comfortable on the mattress: her legs outstretched, back resting against the wall, and the book in her lap.

"Are you sure you do not want to rest?" the professor glanced at Saima's reflection in the mirror next to his desk.

"No, I am good," came the pat response from Saima, her eyes were already scanning a page.

Narayan Shastri orchestrated with his fingers on the glowing screen of the iPad; touching the display at certain points, sliding left, then right, moving his fingers up and down. A mural of Akbar presiding over his court came up on the screen. "We are looking for clues pointing to Akbar and his…," Narayan turned to look at Saima; she had fallen asleep with the book resting next to her. Shastri got up from his desk, walked lightly towards the sleeping figure, pulled the blanket over her, picked the book up, and kept it back on the shelf. He returned to the desk, the image of Akbar's court displayed on the screen. The professor looked at the image, then leaned back and closed his eyes.

Narayan allowed himself to submerge deep inside the image. As time ticked away on a wall clock in the room, he felt as he had been transported into the still image. His mind's eye wandered around the image. He could see Akbar – in his regal robe studded with precious stones glittering red, green and blue, sitting on his plush seat of throne covered with delicate cushions and embellished with intricate artistry, fanned by servants holding peacock-feather fans – listening patiently to a courtier while keeping an eye on the audience. The audience was seated in two neatly divided rows with the emperor at the head. Shastri observed that the gathering was made up of people of different faiths and beliefs. Each member wore a distinct robe and colour, different from the rest. From where Akbar sat, Narayan could see the different colours, different robes, and the different sects being amalgamated into one whole. Probably this is why Jalal-ud-Din Mohammed Akbar strove to unite the different fragments of religion, caste, and creed to reflect a singular vision.

The professor's mind then drifted to a second mural of Humayun ruling over his court. The emperor too was among courtiers, presiding over affairs, listening to them patiently. The emperor had an attentive expression: lips together, hands perched one on top of the other, ears wide open and tuned to the present, eyes focused but maintaining a soft gaze.

This image of Humayun faded into Akbar heading his court, whose disposition was a mirror reflection of his father. The son, in a way, had become his father.

He opened his eyes, a glimmer of a clue hung in the threads of Narayan's mind. The professor had to just reach for it and grab it. Narayan tried and focused his eyes on Akbar's mural again. It had been a long day, but the professor felt that he just needed one final push of his focus.

Narayan concentrated and could see the various religious heads sitting around Akbar in the mural. The secular emperor had a penchant for holding discourses with people heading different religions in an effort to increase his understanding and knowledge of the different faiths under his rule. There was one member in the mural that seemed like an anomaly: A man with milk white skin, a golden cross hanging around his neck, wearing a navy blue cassock contrasted with a pearl-white clerical collar. *A Christian priest, maybe from Europe*...thought Shastri. This observation lit up a recess of his memory. He quickly brought forth an image of a letter with quick touches on his tablet slate. The letter contained Roman English script etched in calligraphy with the Mughal alam[5] – a rising sun eclipsed by a crouching lion – stamped on its masthead. Narayan's eyes read: "*As most men are fettered by bonds of tradition, and by imitating ways followed by their fathers... everyone continues, without investigating their arguments*

[5] Flag sign

and reasons, to follow the religion in which he was born and educated, thus excluding himself from the possibility of ascertaining the truth, which is the noblest aim of the human intellect. Therefore we associate at convenient seasons with learned men of all religions, thus deriving profit from their exquisite discourses and exalted aspirations."

The professor leaned back on his cushion chair and rocked gently, back and forth. This letter had travelled from the royal court of Akbar to the European court of King Philip II of Spain, circa 1582. In the mural, the priest dressed in navy blue cassock was sent from Spain in response to Akbar's request.

Narayan returned to the mural, it flashed on the screen. Narayan caught sight of an object in the image, placed next to Akbar. The object was emerald green in colour and had a script written on it. Narayan Shastri's eyes illuminated at the discovery: it was Object No. 27. *A place where I read in the light of stars...* the professor repeated and closed and his eyes, brows furrowed. The mind began to draw parallels: *Humayun...Akbar...father... son...Object No. 27...read...library... bonds of tradition... imitating ways...Sher-e-Mandal...library...Akbar...*

Narayan opened his eyes, the brows relaxed. He knew the location of the lock.

Captain Veer lowered his head and placed a soft kiss on a tender forehead. His daughter was fast asleep, snuggled under a warm, pink blanket portraying her favourite cartoon character. He walked out of the room, leaving the door slightly ajar for a thin strip of light: a sword to fight against the dark knight and defend the sleeping innocent.

He walked to the dining table where Swati, his wife, laid out his dinner plate and proceeded to serve steamed white rice, fried dal curry, and roasted potato garnished with coriander leaves. Veer sat down at the head of the table and took a deep breath inhaling the aroma wafting from his dinner plate. He looked at his wife, took her right hand in his palm and kissed it. "This smells absolutely delicious."

Veer began tucking in the serving with great relish.

"When you told me that you will be home for dinner, I wanted to make your favourite dishes," Swati gazed at her husband, her eyes reflecting a sense of longing, then content. "It has been a long time since you have been home for dinner."

Veer swallowed a morsel, "Work's been non-stop," he looked at his wife, "I am sorry…,"

"Come on, Veer…you don't need to apologize," Swati quickly cut short the apology.

Veer mixed a little bit of rice with dal and scooped it with his spoon. He brought the spoon to his wife's lips.

"I am fasting today…dummy."

"Oh," the Captain grinned sheepishly and quickly retraced the spoon's path back to his plate. "Fasting to appease God…or fasting to lose weight?"

Swati contorted her face to demonstrate mock anger and hit her husband's shoulder in a playful manner.

The clock struck ten; Swati loaded the dishes in a dishwasher and turned it on. Veer tiptoed in to the kitchen and hugged his wife from behind, planting a kiss on the back of her neck. Tiny strands of hair on Swati's neck stood to attention. Swati peered into her husband's eyes as the dishwasher hummed its tune.

Major Rathore stepped into a room filled with darkness and silence. For a moment, his body felt paralyzed in the vacuum. Tension gripped over each fibre as the officer's heartbeat raced. Finding the last remaining reserve of sanity, Avinash willed his left hand to lift and turn on a switch. White, halogen light flooded the room dispelling the darkness, and the tension. The heartbeat began pumping at a normal rate once again.

A dining table with two chairs parked in the space between it, greeted the officer's eyes. Habit took over the motor reflexes of Avinash as he walked to the kitchen, pulled open the handle of a cream-coloured double door fridge, reached for a microwave-friendly square-shaped container, placed the container in the microwave and set it for two minutes. Droplets of steam formed underneath the lid of the container, as it rotated clockwise inside the oven, indicating the food has been warmed. Handle of the microwave pulled open and the officer carefully removed his meal. A chair parked on the left-hand side of the dining table slid out. Avinash sat down, paid his respects to the meal in front of him with a silent prayer, and slowly opened the container. Grabbing a steel spoon from a stand kept on the table, Avinash proceeded with his meal. The Major kept his shoes on while he ate. For a while now, the shoes had performed the role of his dinner companion.

Thick, wavy steam wafted from rich brown brew of coffee filled neatly in a mug. The steam flickered over the tip of Saima's nose. Her eyes opened slowly bringing to focus the cup. Her mouth parted to greet the morning with a yawn. The professor was at his desk with his eyes on his iPad and a cup of coffee in his left hand. Saima lifted her body up from the mattress and rested her head on the adjacent wall.

"Were you awake all night?" Saima asked, clearing her throat.

"Good morning. Did you sleep well?" Narayan turned his attention to Saima. She nodded her head 'yes' while trying to suppress another yawn with her right hand.

Her deep brown eyes tried to register the room; it looked different. Maybe the stream of light filtering in through a single pane window placed behind the professor. The study was small, but maximized its space with minimal furniture, giving it an easy and relaxed décor.

"Narayan...I had the strangest of dreams yesterday night."

"Yeah..."

Saima took a sip of coffee and closed her eyes for an instant trying to feel the first kick of energy delivered by the brew. "A courtesan was lying in the lap of her lover, a prince...I guess. The setting was a royal garden in the bloom of spring. The two lovers were lost in themselves, and lost to the world around them," Saima took another sip, "A man barges in; he is probably the father of the prince. He removes his sword from its sheath, raises it up in the air and brings it down on the two lovers. The sword hits empty ground, as the lovers transform into white doves and fly away."

"Hmm," Narayan rubbed his chin, which sported a faint stubble. "Looks like the Mughals have had their effect on you."

"You don't say," Saima dipped her lips to the rim of the mug and sipped. "This coffee's damn good. I am beginning to envy you."

The professor was engrossed with his tablet slate.

"Did you sleep at all?" Saima repeated her earlier question.

"I got a few hours of shut eye," replied Shastri catching Saima's reflection in the mirror close to his desk. "By the way, Object No. 27, our precious key, has found its lock."

Saima tried to make sense of what the professor had just said. A few seconds passed before it dawned on her. A smile broke on her face, "You found the lock. This is not good, it is great! So, tell me, where is it."

"Fettered by bonds of tradition," Narayan read from the letter on the screen, "imitating ways followed by their fathers," Saima leaned forward with the coffee mug clasped in her hands, hanging on to every word, "Humayun gazed at stars and read in Sher-e-Mandal...Akbar was his son... imitating ways followed by their fathers..."

"Akbar too had a library," Saima slowly unwrapped the riddle.

"Yes, Lodi Garden."

"Lodi Garden," Saima kept her right thumb and index finger on her forehead and as if trying to extract a piece of information from her memory. "But Lodi Garden houses tombs and mosques, if I am not mistaken."

"You are right," Narayan's eyes reflected a hint of surprise at the fact that Saima knew about it.

"Tombs and mosques belonging to," Saima paused for recollection, "belonging to the Sayyid and Lodi dynasty." She took a large sip of coffee as an award for her effort.

"Very good," Narayan nodded his head, with a hint of professor-esque tone in his voice. "When the Mughals began their rule, they would modify the landscape of the gardens, by constructing structures and towers, to suit their particular needs. Akbar used Lodi Garden as a library cum observatory, like his father Humayun, to store important documents."

"Where is this library slash observatory located in the garden?"

Narayan thought for a few seconds, "I don't know."

Saima raised her eyebrows slightly, "I never imagined I would hear that from you. I hope I am not dreaming again."

Narayan took a sip of his coffee and thumbed his iPad; a satellite image of Lodi Garden emerged on screen.

"Does this mean that we have to search each and every structure for the lock?" Saima cleared her throat and threw the question at Narayan.

"No, we can leave out the tombs and mosques and focus our search on the remaining structures, which," the professor peered into the screen, "limits us to just two." Narayan motioned Saima to come over to his desk.

Saima got up from her mattress with the coffee mug in hand, stretched her neck to her left and then to her right in one quick motion to release its tension. She walked over to the desk and peered at the screen.

"This structure here," Shastri pointed to a spot to the right of Mohammed Shah Sayyid's tomb, "and this one here," the second spot was near the Athpula[6] Bridge. "Time to call the two gentlemen at DIA."

Saima took the last remaining sip of her coffee.

Veer felt a soft voice drift in and out of his sleep. He groggily opened his eyes.

"Papa…papa…"

A soft tender voice greeted the officer. His daughter, with two ponytails hanging beside each ear, dressed in her red-check school uniform, was pulling at the blanket that covered Veer.

"Good morning, princess," the officer half yawned as

---

[6] Eight Piered

he greeted his daughter, and embraced her in a bear hug. His daughter wriggled out of his hold and ran to the door of the room.

"Mummy is calling you for breakfast."

"Tell her, daddy will be there soon."

The little girl ran out of the room.

A crisp newspaper folded open. Veer sat at the table having his morning cup of tea and scanning the paper. It was the usual: a daily dose of violence interspersed with politics and sports. The headline about terror suspects arrested in Pune caught his eye. As he read the article, he caught a glimpse of his daughter having toast with jam. The officer began to wonder how the innocence of children evolved into brutality of men. He wondered whether people who carried out terrorist acts had daughters, just as he had; whether they too had dreams for their daughters, just as he had.

Last year's Delhi blasts had brought Veer face to face with an invisible enemy: An enemy that roamed the same streets; ate the same food, dressed the same way as their victims, before unleashing murder. He put the paper down and looked at his wife who brought a glass of chocolate milk for their daughter.

Veer thought about his partner.

Avinash stood in his balcony and took in the sights of a winter morning: bare branches of trees juxtaposed with painted outlines of residential buildings. He took a sip and appreciated his own effort at brewing tea. Making a cup of tea was something he was getting good at, however, he missed his wife's special masala tea.

The Major walked into his living room and turned towards

the kitchen. A framed picture of his wife hung on the wall in the room with two incense sticks burning below it. She had been a victim of the Delhi blasts.

Avinash's phone rang; he rushed out of the kitchen and picked up his mobile phone placed on the dining table.

"Morning Narayan. Okay...sure...that's great news. Will let Veer know about it immediately."

Avinash pressed 2 on his keypad, the phone dialled Veer's number. "Veer...Professor Shastri called..."

8

A thick morning mist hung over the green lawns and brick-coloured tombs and mosques of the serene Lodi Gardens. Faint outlines of people, out for a morning stroll, weaved in and out of the mist. In one corner of the gardens, the outlines were a tad different. Thin antennae stood up from square backpacks framing the shoulders of people. The outlines looked like winter months, with the antennae resembling the proboscis.

Portable radar vision scanners roamed the walls of the first structure, which was a red brick monolith. The scanners had textbook-sized white screens attached to thick black handles. On each scanner, there was a green button located to the right hand side of screen, which served as its power switch. Short-range radar emitted by the scanners produced images of the interior of the monolith in crisp 3D. In case there was something embedded inside the walls, it would show up on screen in its entire outline. The screen would also indicate if the scanner was moving left, right, up, or down with respective blinking arrows. This allowed the team to search for any hidden objects or hidden vaults within the structure in a non-invasive manner. Each scanner could cover an approximate area of 6 feet by 2 feet.

Narayan was once again impressed by the technology possessed by the DIA. He had read in the newspapers a few months ago that radar vision scanner was a prototype developed by a product development and technology-consulting firm based in the UK. Narayan was now seeing the same device in action.

Major Rathore and Captain Veer kept an eagle eye on their team. So far, nothing sensational had developed in the hazy morning.

The structures of Lodi Gardens were under the strict supervision of the Archaeological Survey of India. The two officers had to put in a special request for their team to scan the two structures. The request was granted immediately. Narayan had informed Avinash and Veer about the possibility of the lock, to which Object No. 27 was key, hidden in one of the two structures.

The radar vision scanners moved around the stone structure, slowly, carefully, not missing an inch. Narayan stood a few feet away from the team, his mind ticking away at the possibilities if the lock was discovered. Saima wandered around the coterie of men, lithe as a butterfly, stopping in her stride here and there if something caught her fancy.

"There's nothing here," Major Rathore's voice hung over the group, like the morning haze.

"We should check out the second structure then," Narayan replied.

The group made their way from one corner of the Garden to the other. From an aerial view, the men resembled ant-like figures making their way to their mound. Narayan led the way.

The professor stopped at a monolith structure situated adjacent to Athpula Bridge. The wide, rectangular structure displayed a similar style of architecture, characteristic of the period: built with sandstone bricks and a dome at the top. The only distinctive feature of the structure was that was that there was no point of entry.

The rest of the group streamed around Prof. Shastri.

"Are you sure this is the second structure?" Captain Veer enquired.

Narayan walked to the monolith and began surveying it at close quarters, strolling around it. Major Rathore motioned the team to scan the structure.

The morning sun finally broke through the haze and flooded the scene with a faint yellow glow. X-ray scanners moved around on the walls of the monolith. Nothing came up on the screens for a minute.

Then, one screen began to blip.

Narayan, Saima and the two officers made their way to the beeping screen. One of the bricks indicated an outline of a hollow compartment behind it. The professor looked at the screen, the brick, and shifted his gaze to the two officers. "May I?"

Major Rathore and Captain Veer nodded their heads.

Narayan gently pushed the brick, it moved inwards.

Everyone and everything stood still. Nothing happened for a few seconds.

A puff of air escaped from the base of the structure. "Everyone, move back," Major Rathore alerted the group.

A loud scrunching sound followed the puff of dust. Birds resting on trees nearby flew away fearing danger. The portion of the monolith, which had the hollow brick pressed inwards, slowly rose up. The professor gaped wonderstruck.

The left wall of the monolith rose up a few feet and revealed a point of entry.

"We'll need a flashlight," quipped Captain Veer.

"Wait, I may have a better idea," Narayan walked to a black backpack placed near Major Rathore. He unzipped it, and removed the emerald-green Object No. 27 from it. Rays of the sun were brighter, clearer, allowing parts of the object to glitter. Professor Shastri held the object in his hand and walked to the opening. He stood at the mouth of the opening for a second; Saima and the two officers quickly joined him. The professor bent down from his waist and entered the monolith.

It took a while for the eyes of the four people inside the monolith to adjust to its pitch black darkness. "Maybe the flashlight was a good idea," Saima offered her opinion.

"Wait for it," Narayan Shastri requested.

Object No. 27's green halo slowly illuminated the black space, throwing soft reflection on the surprised faces of the two officers and Saima Azmi. The light illuminated a row of steps leading down. Professor Shastri descended, taking one step at a time. Narayan seemed to be a connecting line between two objects of the past: Object No. 27 in his hands and the flight of stairs beneath his feet. Saima followed Narayan close behind, her left hand holding his right elbow with the lightest of touches. Major Rathore and Captain Veer followed a few steps behind.

As the green light fell on the walls inside the monolith, it reflected a blank canvas. The flight of stairs descended to a dead end, but turned right to reveal a passage. Footsteps echoed across the hall of a narrow passage preceded by the green glow.

The passage carried a scent reminiscent of wet mud; soft echoes of water waving back and forth precipitated at the walls.

"Looks like this passage runs through the bridge," wondered Saima aloud.

"Possible," chimed in Veer.

"Somebody's been here before," Narayan sounded serious.

"Like an emperor or king," Major Rathore replied with a quick smile.

"No, like a person wearing what we are wearing, maybe a couple of hours ago."

"Sounds impossible," Saima opined.

Narayan stopped in his tracks. He directed the green halo to the ground beneath the walls of the passage. It was littered with pebbles and skeletons of leaves. The professor drew the light closer to the strip they were walking on. "If this monolith has been opened right now, after centuries, these pebbles and leaves should have been under our feet as well. Our path, however, is clear, indicating that someone may have cleared it while they undertook an underground expedition."

"Narayan, I beg your pardon, but it sounds farfetched," Major Rathore concluded.

"Okay, let's move on," Narayan walked straight ahead.

The green halo led the professor to a wall at the end of the passage. Narayan scanned the wall with the object. It soon illuminated a cavity in the wall. Narayan peered into the cavity excitedly, with the emerald green light rushing into it. He expected the cavity to reveal something of great significance. What he saw, however, surprised him. Narayan inserted his hand into the cavity and slid out an object, an object that was a piece of modern-day communication: a mobile phone.

"What the...," Captain Veer's voice lost its trail in the darkness.

A palm-sized cell phone sat in the large hands of Major Rathore, its screen reflecting the faces of the officer and Veer. Narayan, Saima, and the two officers had traced their way back outside the monolith structure. The phone was black in colour with blue border. Its screen reflected the soft outdoor sun. The model was one that the present generation would scoff at and consider a relic.

"Maybe Akbar invented the very first cell phone," grinned Captain Veer. Major Rathore continued to look at the screen; the signal strength indicator displayed no bars.

"Wasn't Object No. 27 supposed to unlock something?" Saima asked the professor.

"The object served as a metaphorical key. Its real purpose was to light the way of the passage, and, more importantly, identify the secret cavity. Without the green halo of the object, it would be impossible to know which one is the secret cavity."

"Then, how did the phone reach the cavity?"

Narayan pondered over Saima's question. His thought process was interrupted by the loud ring of a mobile phone. Major Rathore's eyes widened; the phone in his hand was ringing, an unknown number flashed on screen. The officer let the phone ring a couple of times and then pressed the answer button. Narayan and Saima crowded near the Major.

A gruff voice on the phone enquired what the Major and his team were doing at Lodhi Gardens on a cold, winter morning. The Major quickly pressed the speaker button and brought the phone away from his ear.

"You have wasted your morning looking for a clue that leads to the diamond, and that clue is now in my possession. Looks like I will always be a step ahead of you. Good luck finding the diamond. "

"Who is this?" barked Captain Veer.

"The man you have been searching for. And this phone will blow up as soon as I cut the call..."

The line went dead. Avinash Singh immediately flung the phone a few feet away. Everyone backed off. The phone fizzed, sizzled and caught fire, but nothing dramatic happened.

"Chinese mobile, I guess," remarked a team member.

A bird darted across the water stream surrounding the Athpula Bridge creating ripples on its surface.

"Professor, Saima," Captain Veer spoke softly, "Did you, by any chance, mention about this operation to anyone in passing?"

"Just because you are from the DIA doesn't mean the leak, if indeed it occurred, could not have happened from your office," Narayan replied raising the pitch of his voice. "Saima has gambled with her life to get Object No. 27 back to the authorities, and all you have done is suspect her and suspect me of disclosing vital information."

"I am sorry Professor Shastri," Captain Veer sounded genuinely apolegetic, "What I meant to ask came out the wrong way," the Captain lowered his gaze.

"This is a tricky one," Major Rathore put a hand over his partner's shoulder. "No one expected Major Salim Khan to pull a fast one on us," the Major gently patted Veer's shoulder.

The bird darted across the water and perched itself on a tree, overlooking the group of people.

Major Rathore looked at Narayan and Saima, "But, I believe Major Khan has done us a great service."

Puzzled expressions greeted the officer.

"Now we know why Major Khan is here and his connection with Object No. 27. He is searching for the mystery diamond, mentioned in Humayun's letter to Akbar. That was why he stole the object from Purana Qila," Major Rathore explained. "All that we need to do now is find our next clue. Narayan, any ideas?"

Narayan wrestled with a thought; a thought that seemed a likely solution in this situation. It was, however, a solution which was not an easy one for the professor. "There is one person," everyone looked at Shastri, "who can help us out…Lieutenant General Shastri, my father."

9

The Diamond - I

Still, clear skies stare down the plains with a blank expression. An orange sun peaks its eager head gently above the horizon. Dust resting on the ground lifts up with a gentle wind, the dust blows across the feet of men standing upright with spears by their side. A vast expanse of men, horses, and elephants stare at an opposition, made up of a relatively smaller number of man and beast. Men shift their weight from one foot to another, horses flick their ears driving away imaginary flies, elephants swing their trunks like a clock's pendulum: the relative uneasiness before the birth of battle. Buoyed by their numbers, the vast expanse bears its arms with a will to crush the enemy and once again reign supreme. There is, however, one thing that creates a sense of discomfort amongst this sea of men - hard and clear reflections of the sun striking straight across the plain from hollow metallic mouths attached to wooden wheels. No one knows what these mouths are capable of spitting out.

The commander of the smaller army sports a wry smile. Numbers of the opposition wouldn't mean much once he unravels his strategy on the battlefield. A strategy that would allow the commander to herald a new beginning, albeit a glorious one, that will be remembered as long as the mechanics of time tick in motion.

Gliding across the clear sky, like a black dot on white, a bird of prey slides nonchalantly: Instincts tell the bird that a feast of dead flesh and blood would soon be laid out on the plain.

Nothing moves. The two, albeit mismatched armies stand on ceremony, waiting, sizing up each other.

And then it begins. A single arrow flies from one end of the field, and pierces the enemy ranks. It pierces the white, membranous eye socket of a foot soldier, and breaks open a portion of his skull. Bright red blood oozes out from the eye socket and drips on the dusty plain.

Blood marks the beginning.

A battle cry rushes across the plains, deafening the silence surrounding it. Man and animal peel away from the vast expanse and stride forward, then break into a run; weapons pointed straight at the enemy's heart. The commander merely looks on, waiting for his moment. Tension grips the hands of his army, as they clutch their sharpened weapons, ready to strike. A few of them glance at their commander for a sign. The enemy is at striking distance, roaring, growling, and closing in with every heartbeat. The eyes of the commander twinkle; the enemy has baited his trap. No mortal being can stop his victory now. He closes his eyes for an instant and sends a silent prayer to the almighty force of creation. His eyes open, his hands are raised; the central flank sets into motion, bursting forth to meet the enemy head on. The ground shudders with the footfall of men and beasts, each trying to strike the first blow. Defeat and victory no longer on their minds; just the basic instinct of killing to survive.

The battle crowns its head from the flat belly of the plains, the two armies its midwife.

Bone crushes against bone, flesh cuts through flesh, spears dig into limbs separating tissue from membrane, swords shred steeled-armour, and courage. Dust of the plain rises up, cloaking the macabre dance of death from the clear eyes of the sky. Ears are sliced and fall to the ground, fingers are severed and hang from their joints, legs are trampled upon and pounded to fine pulp, heads neatly separated from necks. Blood oozes, blood splatters, blood leaks, blood is spit out. Soldiers, silhouetted against the rising curtain of brown dust, drive their swords into each other's gut. Arrows fly across the plains, in a deluge, blotting out the sun. A battle-axe cuts through the legs of a brown stallion bringing its rider crashing to the ground. The rider, trapped under the dead horse, is unable to defend or attack. His hapless expression is reflected on the blood-tinged axe before it comes down, slicing the belly of the rider in one swift stroke, halving it. A red pool drenches the two bodies, of the horse and its rider, creating a liquid perimeter. The thick head of a mace thuds into thighs of an enemy soldier. The soldier falls to ground, his spit and blood mixing with the dust of the earth. He grits his teeth, particles of dust lodged between them, raises his scimitar and gets up from the ground limping. The soldier drives his weapon into the shoulder of his enemy carrying the mace and tears through its ligaments.

The brown earth slowly transforms into a red, wet stream.

The vast expanse commits more men and beast to the cause: Flood the enemy with its numbers and suffocate their will. The opposing commander smiles, this is his moment. He raises his hand. The left and right flanks of his battalion break forth. As the next wave of the vast expanse surge and crash into the sea of men in the middle, the right and left flanks attack from the periphery driving the fresh wave of their enemy's attack into the centre, trapping them. Pieces of steel armour, dispatched by a sword, fly across the air and pierce the Adam's apple of a lanky foot soldier. Thick red fluid springs out colouring the cheek of a fellow soldier battling for survival with his spear. The flanks grind inward, slashing through a sea of skin and armour.

The plain gives one final thrust to push the battle out of its belly, so that it can be peaceful and tranquil once again.

With its patience wearing thin, the vast expanse mounts their final assault. Victory will surely be theirs. Broad, heavy feet of elephants set forth on the plains crushing the enemy's charge. The earth trembles under the weight of the marauding horde of battle-hardened beasts; leaves of a tree on the outskirt of the plain shake and quiver due to the impact of the new force. The opposing commander raises his sword and rides out. The time has come to reveal the final attack. His men guarding the cannons set fire to the wicks. Swell of the muzzle spits out black cannon balls hurtling them deep into enemy territory. The black metal balls fly through the sky with the commander tearing through the plains below. Cannon balls drop down and tear through man and beast alike. The inanimate metal does not differentiate between friend and foe. It simply destroys, tearing through membrane, artery, and vein; splattering blood like monsoon rain.

Echoes of the balls of fire, alien to the elephants, drive the animals into frenzy; their minds scrambled. Unable to bear the shrieks of the flying metal balls, the agitated elephants charge their own lines, crushing their own army, trumpeting wildly.

Hooves of a horse rise from the ground as its rider stab his spear through an elephant's trunk, bringing the animal to its knees. The mahout jumps and runs away only to be a mark for a bouquet of arrows that punctures every fibre in his body.

Surrounded in the centre of the battlefield, without any space to reroute and regroup, men and beast of the vast expanse are shredded, cut, and chopped, like tender juicy pieces of meat at the hands of an expert butcher. The battle strategy of one man, the commander, seemed to be overpowering the numerical might of the expanse.

The commander enters the heart of the battle riding on his white stallion. Without pausing, he cuts through the field in a straight line. Untouchable, like a streak of white lightning, the commander scissors through the enemy. His sword moves through bodies of man and animal, as if merely cutting a clear path through a weeded forest.

The commander traces a line from his end of the battlefield to the enemy's end. He brings his horse to a halt and looks back. His ears catch cries of victory: the enemy has succumbed. The head of his adversary, decapitated, bobs up on down on a spear. The vast expanse disintegrates. What was a surge now drips away through the cracks: men running away, abandoning their common goal.

Victory is his[7].

The sun rests high in the sky. Dust settles back on the plain, peaceful, tranquil.

Flies circle around an animal's intestine, coloured pink, spilled out. The bird of prey swoops down. It settles besides its meal and digs its curved black beak into the feast.

Footsteps form on the earth, wet and heavy from blood spilled for victory. The commander walks through the plain, his senses numb to the savagery of battle, his spirit rejoicing in triumph. Deputies of the commander hold his hand as he passes them and congratulates him. His eyes look up and close for an instant, thanking the Almighty.

The plains witness the birth of a new dynasty.

Echoes of horses trotting on cobbled streets ring through narrow lanes of the ancient city. The victorious march to claim what is rightfully theirs – the throne of the defeated. Curious eyes peek out of their sheltered roofs. There is no grand ovation, no yellow flowers of marigold dropping from the skies, no cries of "long live the king", simply a sense of anxious trepidation that cloaks the victory march. A kid tries to run with the marching men, but is yanked inside by his stern mother.

An open, deserted gate of a redbrick fort towers over the commander and his coterie, greeting them. The men enter inside the hollow corridors with a swagger that seemed to suggest that the fort had been theirs by birthright. Eyes of the commander keenly search for the gold and jewellery hidden inside secret chambers in the belly of the fort. No victory is complete without securing the wealth of the defeated.

---

[7] Babur's victory in the First Battle of Panipat (1526)

A wooden door creaks on its hinges; heavy shoulders barge against it asserting their strength on the door, trying to break it open. The door gives way, its hinges uprooted. Black pupils of the men's eyes bathe in the golden glow of the vast, dark room: Golden bricks cover its walls; gold coins, gold bars, and gold jewellery cover its floor, heaped on in layers.

Amidst the golden glare, a single beam of white light rises from the depth of layers of gold and shines through hitting the room's dome ceiling.

The commander's eyes widen; something tells him the white light is what he has been searching for. He steps inside the room and wades in gold, reaching the white light. Fingertips dip inside the layers of wealth and search. A hard object hits the fingertips, different from the bullion flowing around the room. The commander lifts the object, pieces of gold slide away revealing the white, shimmering crown of a diamond. Nestled in his palm, the precious stone rises up revealing its magnificent glory, flooding the room in its luminescence, outshining the gold.

The commander relaxes, a sense of his destiny uniting with his spirit surges through his veins. At peace, he looks at the large, shining diamond, and feels like the emperor of the universe.

An empty teacup sat still on top of a glass table. A hand, softened by age but steady in its grip, extended a wooden smoking pipe to an ashtray placed next to the teacup on the glass table. Rotating the bowl of the pipe to face the ashtray, long, thick fingers tapped it gently. The glass table caught the reflection of a square-shaped, clean-shaven face sporting a neatly trimmed moustache. Lieutenant General Madan Shastri, who had retired from the army a few years ago, brought out a pouch containing blended tobacco from the pocket of his trousers. Laying the pipe on the table, with its bowl resting on the ashtray, the retired army man pinched a thumb full of tobacco. The letter 'S' was imprinted on the bowl in gold.

Though Madan Shastri had retired from active services, he did not lead the life of a retiree by any stretch of the imagination. Days were spent applying his years of experience to help intelligence agencies, such as the DIA, protect the diverse and varied land of people and cultures, which he always referred to as Bharat, and never as India. Most people, especially his superiors, dismissed this particular quirk as a one off, but Madan Shastri had a valid reason for referring to his country by its self-ascribed Sanskrit name rather than its English version: Why associate the name of my country with its colonial past.

The retired lieutenant general would tap into his contacts, at administrative level and street level, to gather critical information which would deter enemies of the state, who roamed openly on streets and struck terror as per their whim and fancy depriving innocents of a future. He had worked out a vital lead in the Delhi blasts, and passed on the information to respective agencies and authorities. The information, however, lost its voice amongst the multitude of information that streams in every single day.

Madan Shastri was highly respected in intelligence circles and was treated with reverence whenever he chose to make an appearance. The DIA headquarter was abuzz the previous day when he paid a visit to Major Rathore and Captain Veer. Each and every member of the staff rose to their feet, like pupils greeting their teacher, when he entered the bureau.

When Major Salim Khan was mentioned, Madan Shastri's mind started ticking about the various possibilities. One thing was sure: terror was just around the corner. He was convinced that the retired ISI officer could not be in New Delhi for anything except taking lives. Captain Veer mentioned about the Taj Mahal visit by an ex US President. Madan Shastri felt it could be a cause for concern and advised the DIA officers to beef up security. In the meanwhile, he would gather any information he could lay his hands on and pass it to the two officers.

When Major Rathore had spoken to lieutenant general Shastri the previous morning about the disappearance of a Mughal artefact, the retired army man could not resist suggesting Narayan's name. Madan Shastri hoped that he would come face to face with his son during the course of the investigation. It had been a long time since he had seen Narayan; the last time they met was when his wife, Narayan's mother, had passed away.

With the bowl of his pipe neatly filled with dried tobacco, Madan Shastri placed its tip in his mouth and took a test draw. Satisfied, he lit his pipe with a black, matte-finished lighter. His cheeks instinctively drew in the smoke and released it, slowly. The body relaxed, his eyes softened, his shoulders arched back on a cushioned cane chair; but his lips hungered for another draw of tobacco. Smoke from the pipe stretched out in a straight line upwards and dissipated into the still, winter morning.

He glanced at his teacup on the table. The colours of the cup had faded away in a graceful manner, revealing its age. Washed out colours of a rainbow ran around the cup in a circular fashion. His eyes wrinkled slightly as a memory associated with the cup streamed into him like tobacco smoke streamed into his lungs: He had strongly protested being served tea in a rainbow coloured cup. Mrs. Shastri coaxed and cajoled him with the argument that a little bit of colour would do no harm to one's cup of tea.

Just as the colours of the cup had faded with time, Madan Shastri felt his life too was fading away.

He took a second, long drag from the pipe and released it from the corners of his mouth. He glanced at his steel-coloured wristwatch. Time seemed to be moving a tad slower than it did when the teacup had all its colours intact.

Narayan pushed open a wrought iron gate and stepped on to a cobbled path, which neatly divided a rectangular patch of finely manicured lawn. The white cobbled street, in a straight line, between two patches of green grass on either side reminded the professor of his hairstyle as a young kid: hair partitioned at the centre, falling out sideways. Memories of his mother carrying a plate of steamed rice mixed with yellow dal and rolled into round portions, chasing a young Narayan clad only in white underwear, tearing across the lawn, flashed across the professor's eyes. This memory was followed by another where he had hurt his knee on the cobbled path, and as drops of red blood dripped on the white path, his mother rushed to pick him up and soothe her crying child. The memories faded and Narayan focused his eyes once again on the present.

He led Saima and the two officers across the lawn, into the spacious interiors of a single-storeyed house, walls of which had numerous gold-polished plaques and pictures of Lieutenant General Madan Shastri receiving medals from the Chief Minister, Defence Minister, and Prime Minister.

Madan Shastri's ears picked up the sound of approaching footsteps. He turned back, his eyes soaking in the presence of his son. Narayan walked past his father, without acknowledging his presence, and took a seat on a cushioned cane chair to his left. Major Rathore and Captain Veer saluted lieutenant general before taking their seats to his right. Saima offered a Namaste and sat facing the retired army man.

"Thank you for seeing us on short notice, sir," Avinash leaned towards the head of the gathering. Madan Shastri turned his glance away from his son, who was lost in thought, and acknowledged the Major. "No need for formalities, Major Rathore. Captain Veer has already briefed me about the situation. How may I be of help?"

"Could you offer us any clues on finding this mystery diamond? We came close, but Major Khan was a step ahead of us."

Madan Shastri took a drag from his pipe and exhaled, "As you all know, my son's the history expert."

Narayan glanced sceptically at his father.

"There is, however, an incident, that could offer a clue."

Madan Shastri took a couple of seconds to gather his thoughts.

"I had been to London last month. A rare artefacts collector, who knew Narayan's mother, had requested my assistance in checking the authenticity of a Mughal manuscript," the lieutenant general conducted the conversation with the pipe, in his left hand, moving like the baton of a Kapellmeister. "This acquaintance was in the process of acquiring the manuscript from a man whose grandfather had served under the East India Company."

Narayan, Saima, and the two officers listened in rapt attention.

"Not many people know this, but I have had a secret hobby of checking and verifying antiquated manuscripts and documents, especially of the Mughal era. Trained partly by my wife, I educated myself in the different types of papers, ink, font styles, and semantics used during the various reigns, from Babur to Aurangazeb."

A look of surprise crossed Narayan's face. His father, a strict disciplinarian, indulging in a hobby, that too of an academic kind, was too much information to process. The professor pinched himself to test whether he was awake or in the middle of a dream.

Veer instinctively glanced at his watch, which caught the eye of Madan Shastri.

"But I digress...To cut a short story shorter, I checked the manuscript; it was genuine."

Madan Shastri brought the pipe back to his mouth and took a drag. "When Captain Veer called me earlier, instinct told me the aforesaid manuscript could be of use to you."

Madan Shastri brought forth a thin, brown folder which he had kept on his right-hand side, in the chair. The file opened and revealed a gleaming, white manuscript ensconced in protective plastic film.

"Narayan, you should take a look at this."

The professor reached out and gently lifted the plastic film from the folder as if it were the most precious thing on earth. Saima leaned in closer to Narayan, her eyes scanning the Farsi text written in black ink.

"How did you manage to get your hands on this manuscript?" Captain Veer enquired.

"The acquaintance who bought the manuscript lives in the neighbourhood. Without hesitation, he lent his prized possession. He was only glad to help out."

Narayan read the manuscript:

I was not my father's favourite son. Call it impatience of youth, or its folly, but I stood up for what I believed in, fought for what was rightfully mine, and that made me, his eldest son, a person my father could never love. Of this, I have no regrets. My respect will, forever, stay with him.

I realize now the hurt and pain I must have caused him when he had to face his own son on a battlefield. Maybe the price I had to pay for my action was to face my own son on the battlefield.

My rebellious nature drew him closer to my son, Khurram. Father saw a future ruler in my son; so do I. He sensed that Khurram would one day extend the glory of our family to great heights; so do I.

Because of his fondness for his grandson, he did reveal our family's secret to him: The one thing which is most pious to our lineage, and the empire. When Khurram later brought the sacred stone in my presence, its divine light held me spellbound. My son tells me that he had to shake me off my stupor. The stone's power to hook your attention immediately reminded me of my most beloved, my queen Noor Jahan.

I named the stone after her: Noor-e-Jahan and offered the most sacred stone of our family to the most precious person.

"Narayan…what do you think?"

Narayan looked up from the document at the two officers, avoiding his father's eyes. "This is very interesting," he said pointing to the manuscript. "Like his predecessors, Jahangir too maintained a habit of penning down his thoughts over a period of time, which would then become his autobiography. Like the *Baburnama* and *Akbarnama*, *Tuzuk-e-Jahangiri* is…"

"…Jahangir's autobiography," Saima completed Narayan's sentence.

A gentle smile broke on Madan Shastri's face.

"How can you be so sure this manuscript belonged to Jahangir?" Captain Veer met Narayan's gaze.

"I am glad you asked. Like I said before, this manuscript is a record of the thoughts Jahangir penned down. There is a mention of Khurram here, which refers to Shah Jahan, Jahangir's son. The emperor talks about his frosty relationship with his father, Akbar…"

Madan Shastri drew on his pipe.

"…This was primarily caused due to his revolt to usurp the throne as a teenager. Jahangir fought a battle with Akbar, but was defeated. In time, he was made emperor. Call it an irony of fate, but just as Jahangir revolted against his father, his eldest son too revolted against him and was crushed in battle."

"Is there anything you don't know?' asked Saima, genuinely impressed.

Narayan smiled and continued, "Now, Akbar was fond of Shah Jahan. The great emperor probably passed on the family secret to Shah Jahan, instead of Jahangir. But the secret did find its way to Jahangir, who named the diamond after his beloved wife…"

"Noor Jahan…" chimed Saima.

Narayan nodded his head, "Emperor Jahangir named the diamond Noor-e-Jahan…Light of the world…"

Major Rathore let out a clap, "Bravo professor, simply superb."

Narayan handed the manuscript back to his father without looking at him.

"Has this manuscript been published as a part of the autobiography?"

"I don't think Jahangir would have revealed this bit of information to anyone, except himself," the professor replied to Captain Veer's query.

"Well...we know now the back story of the mystery diamond; that it passed from Akbar to Shah Jahan to Jahangir to Noor Jahan; that it has a name, but we are still stuck at a dead end," opined Major Rathore.

A pall of silence hung uneasily over the gathering.

"May I suggest something?" the baritone of Madan Shastri drew the attention of the gathering to him. "Narayan's grandfather, my wife's father, was the director of Archaeological Survey of India. He currently resides in Agra. Now that you know the name of the diamond and its lineage, I think you should pay him a visit. He has access to a sea of information regarding Indian History, specifically the Mughal Period. His name is Dr. Lalit Sharma."

"Thank you Sir," Captain Veer got up from his chair, "I believe that is what we will do."

Major Rathore, Saima, and Narayan got up from their seats.

"How is Operation Lincoln progressing?"

"So far...so good," Major Rathore answered the lieutenant general.

"I would like a word with my son, for a couple of minutes, if it is alright with you."

"Sure, Sir. We will wait in the front yard," Major Rathore saluted Madan Shastri.

"Thanks."

The two officers walked on.

"Saima…isn't that you name?"

Saima smiled and nodded her head.

"You and Narayan make a good team. I hope to see more of you."

She felt her cheeks flush slightly at this remark.

"Thank you, Mr. Shastri. I hope to see you soon too. Goodbye."

Madan Shastri got up from his chair as Saima walked by, the sound of her anklets rustled through the morning air.

The father took his seat; he looked at his son, Narayan who was still standing, and motioned him to sit down using his pipe. An entire minute ticked away without a word being exchanged between father and son. Narayan felt as if an hour had passed by.

"I may not have been the best father to you," Madan Shastri spoke with a hint of emotion. "I do not know whether it is too late to try, but I wish to make an effort to get to know you better."

For the first time since he stepped into his presence, Narayan looked at his father.

"You are the only remaining memory of Laxmi, and I cannot afford to lose you."

Madan Shastri looked at his son, "Once you are done with this mystery diamond chase, why not the two of us catch up over a cup of coffee…"

Narayan adjusted the frame of his spectacles, got up from his seat, and walked by. He took a few steps, and then paused. "I cannot promise you anything, but I will surely try to have that cup of coffee," the professor left the backyard.

A faint smile broke on a father's face, for the first time that day.

As the white DIA sedan rolled out of the front yard with Major Rathore behind its wheels, a pair of eyes, concealed behind a dark shade of sunglasses, followed the car's trail.

Wheels of a black sedan set in motion and drifted away past the wrought iron gate.

10

The black sedan progressed in a stop start manner across a busy market street. Major Khan let his eyes wander, and took in the sights, sounds and smells of a space bustling and spilling over with people going about their daily lives. Fresh fruits of various colours were weighed and sold with women customers expressing their displeasure over either the quality of the fruits or with the price; a kebab shop fried freshly minced pieces of succulent meat, the smoke from the frying pan wafted across, whetting the appetite of many a stranger drawing them closer to the shop with their hands dipping in their pockets to check whether they could afford to indulge in a mid day snack. A man dressed in white, accompanied by a woman dressed in red, sat over a harmonium whose exterior displayed a faded elegance of experience that comes only with age. The woman played the thick keys of the harmonium with her slender fingers as the man extended his arms back and forth in rhythm with the tone and pitch of his voice. Salim Khan's eyes drifted to a thick white column of milk poured in and out from one steel jug to another. To the retired ISI officer it seemed as if the column of milk stood static in space while the steel jugs move up and down, exchanging places.

The sedan ejected itself from the narrow street, turned right and entered a wide, sparsely crowded two-lane road. Numbers, displaying acceleration, shifted constantly on the digital speedometer as the car quickly moved through the lower gears and settled in top gear. A soft reflection of the sedan, cast on the fresh tarmac road, glided on under the mid day sun. Salim Khan felt that the crowded marketplace provided a snapshot of this diverse land: less a melting pot and more a churning of the multitude of humanity.

A row of multi-storeyed buildings came into view as the sedan turned left from the main road. Sparkling streams of a water fountain jetting into the air greeted Salim Khan, who was surprised at the grandeur of the residential apartments before him. He had half expected the meeting to take place in a dimly lit, crowded, probably shabby, living space. Dressed in a back overcoat with a navy blue shawl hanging loosely around his neck, the Pakistani Major stepped out of the car and walked to the reception. His plush leather shoes made a soft squeaking sound as they stepped on to the granite flooring of the reception area. The Major made his way to the elevator door and pressed a gold coloured button. Inside the elevator, Salim Khan removed his sunglasses and packed it neatly in the inner pocket of his overcoat. He checked his watch; it showed 35 minutes past 11. The door of the elevator opened to a thin, long corridor. Turning to his right, the Major walked to a door which had the number 56 on it. A gentle knock brought a pair of footsteps to the door. It opened.

"Major Salim Khan."

The diminutive man, who peered through the gap, pulled the door wide open for the Major to enter. Salim Khan entered, took off his overcoat, handed it to the man who had answered the door and strode into the spacious living room. The decor of the room was minimalistic, bordering on spartan. A green laminated table with steel chairs sat in one corner of the room, next to a wall. The windows of the room did not have any curtains draping it and gave view to bare branches of trees outside. A brown coloured sofa set, sans cushions, sat below the windows. There was nothing in the room that would reveal the identity of its inhabitants – members of a cross-border terrorist organization.

The Major decided to take his seat at the table. He pulled out a chair when a clean shaven man, wearing a blue t-shirt and grey jeans entered the living room. *So...this is the new face of terror... looks like an ordinary guy, dresses as an ordinary guy...*mused Salim Khan. Handshakes were exchanged and the two men sat at the table, a static ceiling-fan the lone spectator. Salim Khan sat with his left leg placed over his right leg, the left knee on top of the right knee. The other man sat with his two legs apart, his hands on his sides, in a relaxed state, facing the Major.

"How did you manage to rent this place?" Salim Khan's low guttural tone broke the room's fragile silence.

"Well...let's say we have benefactors... in oil rich kingdoms... who operate beyond the slender reach of law and justice," replied the man, his dark brown eyes maintaining a steady gaze.

"Why do you ask?"

"No particular reason. I did not expect this," the Major pointed his hand at the room, "that's all."

The man took out a packet of smokes from his jeans pocket and popped a cigarette in his mouth, his lips gently pursed. He offered the open packet to Salim Khan who politely refused with a wave of his hand.

"Mind if I smoke?"

"By all means, go ahead."

A deep yellow flame popped out of a yellow lighter and lit the cigarette tip. Spots of orange flashed across the dried tobacco. The man drew a puff; the Major looked at his watch.

"I assume everything's in place for the celebration?"

Celebration was the code word for their operation. The man nodded, and continued to smoke.

"Do you have the package with you?"

The man pointed at the sofa set and replied, "Have a look."

Salim Khan took a couple of long strides and stood, looking down at the bare structure of a sofa-set without cushions. A white mesh covering the seat of the sofa caught the Major's attention. His fingers reached for the mesh and peeled it open. A hollow cavity beneath the mesh revealed ordinary-looking cans of plastic.

"Impressive."

"Thank you, Janaab. On the outside they look like ordinary plastic containers. On the inside, they are laced with a combustible mixture made up of RDX. The ingredients we have used can be found in any home, in any market place."

"I hope it will light up the night sky..."

The man looked at his slowly burning cigarette, "Would have given you a demonstration right here, but then, neither this room nor the two of us would survive it," he said in a matter of fact tone.

Salim Khan took his seat at the table, "Looks like you are ready. People back home would be very happy to hear about it."

The man took a drag and looked at the ceiling fan, "May I ask you something?"

"Yes."

"Do you really think this jihad we are unleashing is going to serve any real purpose?"

Salim Khan looked at the man intently.

"We take lives, which are supposed to be retribution for the lives that they take. So, if we continue to take lives, will it stop them from taking lives that are dear to us?"

Salim Khan crossed his arms at his chest.

"When the bricks of my house melted in the fire caused by shelling, I knew that I had to take lives to have a certain amount of peace. Otherwise, I would go mad..."

The man tapped his cigarette; flakes of ash fell to the ground, "Have you ever felt the need to take a life in order to have peace?"

Salim Khan looked at the man who continued to stare at the ceiling fan. The Major realized it was a rhetorical question. It had, however, reminded him of the time he had lost someone who meant everything to him. How he had lost his grip on reality. Back then, he had wanted to take a life, any life.

"Are you planning to pull out of this operation?" Salim Khan leaned slightly forward.

A smile cracked on the man's face, "No, never. I may have become a man-eating tiger who needs to kill. Without it, I will not survive. And I want to survive...survive for the family who melted in the fire along with the bricks."

The man tapped his cigarette.

Salim Khan took out a brown envelope from his trouser pocket and placed it on the table.

The man took out a USB drive and placed it on the table. Salim Khan took the drive and held it in his hand.

"Head wants you to have it. Some kind of statement of purpose outlining our tactics for the future. Do pass it on to your people."

The Major placed it in his shirt pocket.

"Wait a minute. Will you...I will be right back," the man got up and left the room.

Salim Khan did not know what to make of the person he had just met. Then again, he did not have to. All that the Major had to do was ensure 'Celebration' was executed according to plan. He observed that a half-smoked cigarette was stubbed on the floor. The diminutive man made an appearance, picked the stub and the ash surrounding it with a piece of cloth and exited the room.

Plastic covers of pirated DVDs drew the Major's attention once again to the man who had entered the room. The DVDs were of the latest Bollywood films.

"Would you like to take some for your kids or friends?"

"No, thank you," replied Major Khan.

"Hmm, not a movie buff, are you? Well, merchants of pirated DVDs have been the perfect front for us. Not only have we made a quick buck, we have also been able to plan the entire operation just by selling them to people walking the streets. Somehow, no one here suspects a person who sells movie DVDs. Not even the cops...strange country. If you possess a good collection, they just come pick up what they desire and leave without paying. And the information we got from them in the bargain, through casual conversation, it amazes me."

Salim Khan got up, straightened his trousers, and made his way to the door. The other man continued to sit in his steel chair.

"You know...I figured something out while selling these movie DVDs on the streets."

Salim Khan stopped in his stride.

"This country, on which we have committed and will continue to commit these random acts of terror, it will endure, its people will endure, just as it had in the past. Romans, Mughals, British, Portuguese...they came and they left. So will we," the man lit another cigarette. "This country will survive...," he let out a puff of smoke, "I am not sure we will."

The Major grabbed his overcoat and exited the apartment, the door shut behind him.

Salim Khan shut the passenger door of the sedan. The car began to roll out of the apartment complex. He took out his cell phone and stared at it. The memory of the meeting he just had was a blur, except for words *'felt the need to take a life in order to have peace'* which rang in his ear.

"Salim! Salim! You cannot hide from me forever boy."

The voice rang loud and clear through the courtyard. In the distance, stocks of leaves ripe with wheat swayed gently in the breeze.

A pair of ash-coloured eyes looked through a slit gap along the hinges of a door. The eyes saw a portly woman with thick hands brandishing a wooden stick shaped like a whip. Ten-year-old Salim clutched at the end of his white shirt with his right hand, hoping to gain some sort of strength and composure from what was to follow: the stick whipping across his body until spots of red smudged on the white shirt. He had never seen his mother, the portly woman with the stick, this angry. The innocence of the boy was such that he thought this would probably be his last day alive. His body shivered slightly behind the closed door, perhaps in anticipation of the beating. Shadow of his mother slipped through the gap in the door and cast its looming shadow on the floor of the room. Salim closed his eyes. The boy wished for just one thing: to be alive and breathing after his mother had meted out her punishment.

Earlier that day, Salim had bitten the ear of a classmate. The boy sobbed uncontrollably as blood streamed out of his ear, dripping everywhere, leaving a trail behind. Salim's mother was summoned to the principal's office. With round spectacles resting low on his nose, the principal, a thin wiry man berated the mother for the beastly actions of his boy. It had become a regular fixture in the school now. Just as the moon completed its cycles, Salim would, every now and then, erupt and commit random acts of violence. If not biting ears, then it would be punching a nose, kicking a groin, or piercing the sharp end of a pencil into the soft portion of a thigh. The scrawny principal, looking up from his desk at Salim's mother standing before him with her eyes glued to the floor, asked her why an intelligent boy like Salim (he was their best student) could not control his anger. To Salim's mother, the question seemed like a veiled insult to her lack of parenting. She did not have an answer, no one did. It was this part of her son's character that troubled her to no end. She had taken him to doctors, hakims, fakirs, maulanas...but nothing cured her boy. When it came, the boys' anger unleashed like a torrent.

Whenever Salim indulged in his habitual acts of aggression, it was his father who executed the punishment. The boy did not mind his father lashing at him or bruising him or cursing him or slapping him. A part of the boy seemed to enjoy his father expressing his anger and frustration and looked forward to it. The father was a highly reputed and respected man in the district who headed the local police division.

It was his mother's wrath that Salim feared the most.

The boy and his mother walked from his school to their house. All the way, the mother was silent. Salim knew something was wrong. She was never this silent, the mother always smiled and initiated conversation. Not today. When they reached home, his mother asked him whether he would eat something. The boy nodded. She served him rotis and a bowl of rajma curry. As the boy tucked in his meal sitting crossed leg on the floor, heavy footsteps raged towards him and before the boy could react, the end of a stick whacked across his back. Salim nearly fell on the ground, particles of half chewed food lurching out of his mouth. The boy, however, regained his balance and sprung back on his feet. His eyes widened when he saw his mother, panting like a raging bull, with a stick in her hand. Salim bolted out of the living room, narrowly escaping another whip of the stick. The boy ran as fast as he could into the courtyard, his feet led him instinctively to a store room in the courtyard. He hid in a corner behind its door.

The mother knew where to find him. The boy had a habit of lounging in the store room. Salim would lie on the floor of the room with his feet on the ground and stare at the ceiling. If Salim was not to be found anywhere else, he would invariably be in the store room. His mother had asked him what he did in the room. The boy replied, "Nothing". Ten-year-old Salim found the interiors of the store room the perfect place to relax. All that the room contained were gunny bags of food grains and empty oil canisters. The rich smell of evaporated oil mixed with husky overtones of the gunny bags calmed the boy.

The door of the storage room was pushed open. Echoes of stick burning its mark on tender flesh soon filled the room. The hand did not stop until the stick broke in half.

As the moon sat high in the sky, Salim lay on a cot, face down. Thick, yellow streaks of turmeric paste ran across the various cuts on the boy's back. Patches of dried blood marked the borders of the yellow paste. The mother walked in gently and sat on the edge of the cot. Dry tear lines smudged her cheeks. She kept her hand on the back of the boy's head. Salim smiled.

No one could have predicted that young Salim would change after the birth of his sister, Safi. His occasional bouts of anger subsided. No more incidences of bitten ears, or punched noses, or punctured thighs were reported. The principal began to parade Salim as a role model and a future star who would make his parents, and the district, extremely proud.

As Salim began to devote his time and energy in taking care of Safi, the eccentric parts of his personality, such as lying down and staring at the ceiling of the storage room ebbed. For a reason known best known to Salim, Safi became his centre of the universe. If she cried, he would soothe her; if she was in pain, he tried to make her laugh; if she was hungry, he fed her. The mother would wonder whether Salim was Safi's actual mother and not her.

Safi grew up, and so did Salim's sense of protective love. He orbited her like a satellite. 'Salim satellite' became his nickname, whispered in hush tones, lest he hear it and beat the person to pulp. Though the violence dripped off him, he still had an aura of someone who was not to be messed with.

There was, however, one thing about Salim Khan that troubled his mother.

It was his gaze.

His violent streak had evaporated as drops of morning dew on blades of grass; however, Salim's mother felt a more sinister, albeit silent, force at work. There was no concrete explanation as to why she felt that way; it was just a mother's instinct.

The boy had grown into a young man, tall and lanky. Once, when his father lost his temper with Safi and was about to slap her, Salim came between father and daughter and looked his father in the eye. The mother walked into the living room and stopped in her stride as she saw her son stare down her husband. Her husband was helpless, as if hypnotized by the stare of the young man. The father lowered his gaze.

She called out to Salim and broke the simmering tension in the room. The father walked out of the living room. It was right then her mother's instinct told her that her boy who would innocently feed ants tiny crystals of sugar, was not a boy anymore, not her boy anymore.

Salim Khan knew what he wanted when the time came to ply a trade: he wanted to be a part of the ISI. He believed no other career offered the heady heights of power as the ISI, or Inter-Services Intelligence as was its moniker. The intelligence services in his country had the influence to topple any democratically elected government. It did not bow down to public sentiment; it did not care for what the world thought; the military went ahead and did what they thought was right. It was the ISI that worked behind the scenes, pulled the necessary strings, so that the military could maintain its big brother-like aura.

This suited Salim Khan perfectly.

He passed the entrance test, which tested the candidate's aptitude regarding various analytical abilities and current affairs, and placed in top five percentile. At the interview, he immediately impressed with his clarity of thought. When asked by the man chairing the interview what Salim Khan hoped to achieve with the ISI, the fresh, out-of-college youngster replied, "To free Kashmir from Indian rule."

Salim rose through the ranks like a man who took an elevator, moving up the floors in lightning quick manner. What helped Salim's cause was that he never succumbed to the ego associated with a rising talent. He worked round the clock, was diligent with his reports and submitted them on time, was not afraid to do any kind of work – big or small, and attended social gatherings where military brass interacted with intelligence personnel. All the while, he stayed in the background, confident that his abilities would get him his big break. His peers had begun to talk about his analytical abilities. The man could listen to a couple of intercepts, read a couple of intelligence reports collected from the ground, and formulate a detailed strategy. The strategy would, invariably, lead to a successful mission.

Salim Khan's big break did arrive.

He had been a part of covert operations to supply arms and ammunition to separatist elements threatening to disturb the fragile secular fabric of their neighbour, India. The young officer had worked out a strategy that would never link the intelligence agency to any of the separatist organizations. He however believed that these separatists did not pose a real threat to India. He tried to communicate his opinion to his superiors, basing it on hard facts. Probably because he was too young in the organization to be taken seriously, no one did.

Salim Khan's moment finally came during a dinner gathering between the intelligence agency and top brass of the armed forces. The gathering was held on the lawn of a five star hotel in Lahore. A cool breeze wafted across the sombre gathering bestowing it with a sense of heightened character. Smoke from cigars twirled in the air complemented by quiet conversations. Men, in suits and in uniforms, held on to glasses, some filled with alcohol, some with aerated drinks, as they talked about politics and wars. Streaming waters of a fountain in the centre of the lawn reflected the various colours of decorative lights that were placed around the perimeters of the lawn. Salim Khan stood in a corner and quietly tucked away rajma curry and boiled rice.

"So, you think that our assistance to separatists operating in India is like running a fool's errand?"

The young officer gulped his morsel and looked up. It was the army chief, cigar butting out of his thick lips, a glass of whisky in his right hand, his eyes covered by a pair of Ray Ban aviators even at night.

Salim Khan's throat ran dry, he muttered, "No Sir…the thing is…"

"Speak up boy, I can't hear you," even while speaking in a low tone, the army chief sounded intimidating.

Salim took a deep breath, "Janaab, I believe we need to support those who are capable of making a statement by attacking nerve centres of our democratic neighbour. The elements we now support work on the fringes and will always remain on the fringes."

Some of the men glanced at the young man conversing with the army chief.

"We need to identify organizations that are taking root in Azad Kashmir and lend them our support. They are our future," Salim Khan felt every nerve in his body tense.

"Hmm….," the chief took a puff from his Cuban cigar. The thick lips took a swig of whisky, "Good…," the chief nodded his head and walked away.

For the second time in his life, Salim Khan smiled.

Thus began the young officer's inexorable rise. Salim Khan was soon called to the military headquarters where over a cup of tea with the army chief, he was made part of a special task force within the ISI that would track and handle separatist factions in the Kashmir valley. Their first operation was to provide a safe passage for militants of a separatist faction from Pakistan occupied Kashmir (PoK) to Srinagar. Once the militants made their way to Srinagar, they would be provided arms and ammunition by their handlers. During the operation, Salim Khan displayed keen tactical acumen. It was his suggestion that the militants be armed with automatic guns and grenades only when they reached Srinagar, which proved to be a masterstroke. The militant group was intercepted by an Indian army patrol, but were let off when the group convinced the patrol that they had wandered off in search for their flock of sheep.

The young officer had pre-empted this scenario.

The first mission's success marked the beginning of insurgency and instability in the valley

Salim Khan soon became an integral part of operations that involved arming separatist factions and sending them out into the heartland of their neighbour, who had become a symbol of a successful democratic system. And the continued success of these operations meant that the man continued to grow in stature. Soon, there were Chinese whispers that Salim Khan would one day head the ISI. What worked for the talented officer was his image. He did not indulge in any habits, which would be considered vice in a conservative society. He worked, then went home, and came back to office the next day. Alcohol, cigarettes, women were kept at a safe distance. The man knew that a false step could take him farther and farther away from the one thing he truly coveted: power. Power in the ISI meant being the person who heads it. Another personality trait that worked in favour of Salim Khan was the respect he paid to people around him. It did not matter what their rank or designation was; Salim Khan always had a patient ear and a kind word.

There was, however, a handicap. Salim Khan had never served in the Pakistan army. Unless Khan served in the army and rose to the rank of Lt. General, he would never become the ISI chief.

During one of the dinner gatherings, the army chief brought up the topic with Salim Khan. The young man had transformed from a shy, comfortable-in-the-shadows person, to someone who was not afraid to take centre stage. To the army chief's question, Salim replied confidently, "Then put me on the battlefield. I will give you the years of experience you wish."

The chief offered a wry smile.

Salim Khan soon became a serving officer with the 11th Infantry Division of the IV Corps, which was headquartered in Lahore.

It had been five years year since Salim Khan enlisted in the Pakistan Army. He moved up the ranks in the army unit as well, impressing everyone with his level-headed thinking and limitless courage. Lieutenant Salim Khan was now Major Salim Khan.

Though he was enlisted in the army, Khan continued to work for the ISI, running covert operations and strategizing intelligence gathering. Salim Khan was in his forties now, with grey hair around his temples.

On a hot summer afternoon, Salim Khan's unstoppable march to complete power came to a grinding halt.

He was in his cabin sipping iced tea from a tall glass, which sweated water beads of melting ice, when his mobile phone rang. The voice of his wailing mother greeted Salim. At first, he could hardly make out what she was trying to tell him. Somebody had died, that much he could figure out after a minute, but who...

The words, "Your sister, Safi," caused Salim to freeze. Seconds ticked away on the wall clock; Salim Khan sat frozen in his chair holding the phone to his ear. The mother continued to sob uncontrollably. Salim Khan jolted when another phone in the cabin rang. He picked up the other phone unmindful of the fact that he was listening to his mother sob on his cell phone. The voice over the office phone informed him that a blast had taken place in New Delhi, carried out by separatists. The line then went cold. His mother, between sobs, informed Salim that Safi had died in a blast in New Delhi. The man did not utter a word; neither did he react in any manner. He calmly said goodbye to his mother and disconnected the cell phone.

Salim Khan dialled the army chief, who picked up the phone after a couple of rings. Salim asked the chief whether they had been informed about the blasts in New Delhi. The army chief replied in the negative. Salim disconnected the phone and walked out of his office. He drove to his apartment in the city. Once inside, he locked its doors and windows.

Local police had to be called in later that day when neighbours complained of a man who was shouting and screaming accompanied by loud noises of glasses shattering and furniture smashing against the wall. When two police constables broke into the apartment, their eyes widened at what they saw: Major Salim Khan, a well known figure of the ISI, lying unconscious in a foetal position, shards of glass from windows and mirrors sticking out of his back, broken pieces of wood from doors and shelves scattered around the living room.

The primordial anger, which had been suppressed after the birth of his sister, had erupted inside Salim at the news of her death. The anger had stormed over his apartment, laying it to waste.

A couple of weeks passed by before the army chief visited Salim Khan in the military hospital. When the chief saw Salim Khan lying on his bed, staring at the ceiling, he could not imagine that this was a man who had the world at his fingertips. What he saw now was a shadow of a man he once knew. A fresh, white roll of bandage was wrapped around Salim's forehead. His right arm, which he had fractured during his outburst in his apartment, had been set in cast. The chief took his seat next to the bed and faced Salim, who seemed lost within himself.

"Son, how are you doing?"

The voice snapped Salim Khan out of his reverie and his eyes registered the presence of the army chief. He immediately propped a pillow and sat on the bed with his back resting against the pillow.

"Take it easy," smiled the chief, "I heard about your sister...I am sorry for your loss...," he placed a hand on Salim's shoulder.

"I want you back...Take as much time as you want. Recover, rest, and when you are ready, call me."

The words of the army chief seemed lifeless and empty, even though it was an offering.

A month later, Salim Khan opened the door of his apartment and walked in. Everything seemed exactly the way it was before he had trashed it, as if what had happened was just a dream. His eyes observed a white envelope lying on the centre table; it was from his mother. He opened the envelope and picked out the piece of paper inside it. As he read the piece of paper, Salim was convinced he that this was a dream; the letter read, "Safi is alive."

Major Salim Khan looked at the screen of his cell phone. The sedan was travelling in a straight line across a moderately crowded road. *'Felt the need to take a life in order to have peace'* rang in through his conscious mind one more time. He thought about the effect the loss of his sister had on him, he thought of the reversal when he read the letter from his mother that stated Safi was alive.

Before travelling to India, he contacted the chief and informed him about his trip. The army chief was happy to hear that Salim was up and about and asked him whether he would mind carrying a parcel to be handed over to an acquaintance in New Delhi. Salim Khan had obliged.

As he thought about the interesting exchange he had with the man who had received the packet, the cell phone notified Salim Khan of a text message it had received. The message read: 'Dr. Lalit Sharma, Agra'.

11

Safi Khan grew up under the protective shadow of her brother. Whenever little sister was in trouble, Salim Khan was on hand to help her. In school, there was this particular kid, a rambunctious boy, who believed pestering little girls was a valid form of entertainment. The boy would pull Safi's ponytails, push her around, and poke her with sharp-ended objects.

Salim saw his sister sitting in a corner and sobbing quietly. He comforted her and asked her what was troubling her. With her voice breaking between sobs, Safi told her brother about the boy. Salim comforted her sister and told her not to worry anymore.

When the boy saw Safi at the school playground the next day, he bolted. From that day onwards, no one dared to bother Salim's sister. It seemed to her that Salim was a phantom who had scared the living daylights out of everyone.

Safi drew from the silent, strong personality of her brother and developed a tough-as-nails character of her own, not allowing anyone to dominate her.

Like her brother, Safi too knew what she wanted to do with her life-Study architecture. After completing an undergraduate architecture programme, Safi Khan wanted to go to London to take a master's programme. Her father offered stiff resistance threatening to lock Safi up if she did not get married soon. Salim intervened, and Safi was soon on a flight to the capital city of England.

Safi immersed herself in the architecture and culture of metropolitan London, cherishing every moment she was there. She did not know that soon she would encounter a letter that would change her destiny.

Safi was back home from London for her winter break. Her mother had entrusted her with cleaning the storeroom, a task she did not really relish. Safi would rather have spent time reading one of her architecture books.

Armed with a broom and a mop she set about sweeping the storeroom. As the thick, long bristles of the broom glided across the floor, a haze of dust that streamed out of the door was released. The broom hit the wooden leg of an almirah, knee high.

Safi stopped sweeping and looked at the wooden box, lodged behind sacks of grains and vegetables, its top barely peeping above the sacks. Her hands reached out and lifted the almirah out of its hiding place. She kept it on the floor and sat beside it: The box had intricate carvings resembling a floral pattern. The architecture student ran her fingers over the carvings taking in every detail. Time had marked its march on the almirah: its wooden exterior was faded and worn out.

Safi gently pulled open the doors of the almirah studded with white stones which had lost their lustre. Her hand waded through cobwebs inside it before landing on, what she guessed, was a piece of paper. Using her fingertips, she gently lifted the piece of paper from the floor of the almirah and brought it out. Safi blew away the dust, clinging on to the piece of paper like a long lost lover, to reveal an antiquated letter faded brown with the passage of time. The letter was riddled with holes caused by nibbling insects. Her eyes darted eagerly across the script. It was in Persian, a language Saima had learnt from her mother as a kid.

The Almighty has been generous with me today. Shehenhsah-e-Hind, and my lord, Humayun appointed me as guardian of his son, Jalal. This is an honour and a big responsibility as well, to protect Jalal from his enemies and train him in the art of military warfare. With the blessings of the Almighty, I should be able to transform the boy into a warrior who will establish a firm footing of the Mughal Empire in this land.

The Almighty seems to be genuinely pleased with the life that I lead. I say this because not only did Emperor Humayun trust me with Jalal, he has also trusted me with his family secret.

It is a mystery stone said to be three times bigger than Diamond of Babur. Blessed by a Sufi Saint, this stone has mystical properties; till this stone is in the possession of the Mughals, their dynasty will flourish. I have been trusted with a Key that will unlock the safe containing the diamond. When Jalal comes of age, my lord wants me to pass on the key to him.

I fear that if this key remains in my custody, it will draw the attention of evil eyes in the palace. Since you, my begum, are the one I trust the most, I am sending the 'Key of Fortune' with this letter for safekeeping.

Guard this key as you would your life.

This letter and the key is a secret you must take to your grave.

May the blessings of the Almighty continue to shine on the both of us.

Allah Hafij.

Bairam Khan

Though the letter was faded, torn in a few places, and riddled with holes, the script still stood out making it easy to read.

Safi took a deep breath. She was trying hard to contain her excitement. It seemed incredulous that a letter from the Mughal period, a secret letter which talked about a mystery diamond, was in the storeroom all along. From what she had learnt about the Mughals during her history lessons in school, she drew the connecting line between Bairam Khan, Humayun, and Akbar who was referred to as Jalal in the letter.

Safi Khan felt an irresistible urge to find out more about the mystery diamond. She felt an irresistible urge to answer the call of adventure and mystery that gripped her very soul after reading the letter. At that very instant, the architecture student studying in London, decided to go to New Delhi, seat of the Mughal Empire, and find the diamond. She had the perfect cover for it as well: Her college in London was sending a student delegation to attend an architectural summit, which was taking place in New Delhi in a couple of months.

For the first time in her life, Safi experienced the high of an adrenaline rush.

Later that night, as the two women sat in the courtyard gazing at stars in the clear night sky, Safi Bano asked her mother about an antique wooden almirah. Her mother replied that the almirah belonged to Safi's grandmother, which had been passed on to her by her mother, Safi's great-grandmother. The wooden box was a tradition in the family that passed from mother to daughter. When her mother enquired how she knew about it, the daughter covered her tracks saying she had heard about it from one of their relatives.

"There is, however, a curse attached to the box."

Safi leaned closer to her mother, her curiosity piqued.

"The almirah would be cleaned once in a year by the daughter who possessed it with a blindfold over her eyes. If any mother or daughter were to open the box, it would lead to their death. That is why the daughter who cleans it has her eyes covered with a piece of cloth."

The mother told Safi that the almirah had been misplaced a long time ago. She had tried to search for it but never found it.

"Maybe it is a good thing that the almirah is lost," the mother stroked Safi's head, "It always gave me a sense of dread. I would never want to pass on that cursed thing to you."

Safi Khan was a modern girl who did not believe in old wives' tales. She did not mention her discovery in the storeroom.

12

Major Rathore sipped a steaming cup of masala tea in a brown clay cup. Bright white light, from an incandescent bulb hanging above the officer, reflected off the brown tea on to Avinash's face. Night had fallen on the city. The DIA officer indulged in a hot cup of tea served by a street-side tea vendor. He drank his tea standing on the outer periphery of a narrow, bustling lane filled with eateries. Crowds, composed of various pools – a family of four, a group of six friends, office colleagues – ate, drank, and made merry on a clear winter night. The sounds, smells and smoke emanating from frying pans swirled and mixed, creating a rich amalgamation of colour in contrast to the monotone blue night sky. The officer was on his way back home when he decided to stop by for tea. Narayan and Saima were in Agra and Captain Veer was going over the security details of the US ex-President's visit. This gave Avinash a few hours to kill before turning in for the night. He could not stand the biting loneliness of his two-bedroom apartment and decided to mix with the crowd. As he looked on the various groups chatting, laughing, gesturing, he wondered whether crowds, be it in any part of the world, possessed similar characteristics: The silent one in a group, the talkative one, the one who would laugh boisterously at a joke, the pot bellied uncle or aunty who tucked in as if it was their last meal and the one person who stood outside of it all and observed people; just as Avinash was doing. His eyes locked on a young married couple sharing a plate of steaming hot biryani. The woman was decked in a maroon-coloured sari with silver ornaments, the man was dressed in his finest formal wear. It looked like their first outing together as a married couple. The man leaned over and placed a peck on his woman's left cheek; the woman blushed. Avinash reminisced about the first time he and his wife had gone out to dinner. He could not take his eyes off her the entire night while she played the part of a coy Indian bride to perfection. Later that night, the two of them made love for the first time as husband and wife. Three weeks after they got married.

As the DIA officer drank his tea, the memory of his wife faded and a peculiar sensation engulfed him. It was the feeling that someone was watching him. Avinash caught sight of a bearded face smoking a cigarette from the corner of his eye. The man wore a pathani suit and stood not too far away from him. The officer could not say for sure whether he had seen this person before, but his intuition told him that he had. When the man tilted his cigarette at a particular downward angle to drop the ash off, Avinash knew he had seen this person smoking before. The unusual manner in which the man tilted his cigarette had registered in a corner of the officer's memory which was now coming back to him. This man had been following Major Rathore. The officer had seen this person before when he went to a nearby market, went out for a jog, was standing in his balcony and possibly on his way to DIA as well.

Gulping down the rest of the tea, Major paid the vendor and walked towards the bearded man. The man took a puff and quickly stubbed his cigarette on the street when he saw the officer walking towards him. He took a few steps and turned into the crowd. Avinash quickened his stride.

Mirrors installed in a barbershop caught the reflection of the bearded man hurrying past it; the barber applied thick, white lather on the sunken cheeks of his client and glided his steel razor across it; the same mirrors caught the Major stopping outside the shop, looking around and then walking in the direction of the bearded man.

The white, sports-shoe covered feet of the bearded man mixed alongside leather shoes, heels, canvas shoes, and Hawaiian slippers, navigating through them with agility and speed. The shiny leather shoes of Avinash Singh made its way in a stop start manner across the same pairs of footwear.

Dried red chillies thrown into boiling oil released a puff of smoke silhouetting the visage of the bearded man who walked past the eatery. The Major stopped a few feet away, standing opposite to the puff of smoke, but was not able to see the man's face, obscured by smoke. The man continued walking past the crowd with the DIA officer following him a few yards away. Whenever the Major tried to get a clear sight of his bearded stalker, somebody's head, or face, or hand would come in the way hiding the bearded face. All the while, the officer wondered the number of times he had seen this man.

Major Rathore entered a less crowded lane of the bazaar. His eyes surveyed the area before him. Bright Lights from the bazaar cast its gentle glare on to the street. Clusters of people who had their share of merriment for the night had broken off from the crowd and streamed their way across the street. The long shadow of a man crossing the street glided in front of Major. The officer quickly turned back to catch sight of a brown pathani suit that disappeared into a street corner. Major Rathore began to trot, turned inside the street corner, and ran across its narrow by-lane. When he emerged out of the by-lane, Major found himself to be back where he had started: near the tea vendor. The vendor smiled and asked if the officer had come back for another cup of tea; the officer shock his head while keeping his eyes fixed on the crowd. The bearded man was nowhere to be seen. He took out his phone and dialled Veer's number.

Captain Veer stared hard at the white screen of the laptop; details of the US ex-President's security cordon stared back at him: the number of men who would accompany him from the airport to his hotel, the number of men stationed at the hotel, outside his room, the number of men who would...and the list went on. The officer leaned back on his chair, supported his neck with his palms, and closed his eyes. He knew the entire plan like a kid who knew his nursery rhyme By heart. He opened his eyes, switched off the laptop, got up from his chair, and walked out of the room.

Veer sat beside his daughter's bed and watched his little princess. The sight of his daughter, fast asleep, gave the officer a sense of unadulterated joy and bliss. He patted her hair softly and left her room quietly. Just as Veer closed the door behind him, his phone rang. He answered it instantly; it was Major Rathore.

"Veer...we may have a serious problem on our hands..."

"What happened...? Are you all right sir?"

"I am fine...but I think I am being followed..."

"Ok...have you lost the tail...."

"I tried to follow him, but he vanished...My gut tells me that there may be someone who is keeping tabs on you as well. Watch out."

"Sure...we will talk about it tomorrow morning. Should I come and pick you up?"

"No...I will take a rickshaw and go home. See you tomorrow. Stay alert."

"Yes... good night..."

Veer disconnected the call. He took a deep breath and thought about the phone call. *Is there someone who could be following me?* The officer wondered.

The lights were switched off in the officer's apartment. A bearded figure hidden in the shadows of the night, whose eyes were on the officer's apartment, took out his phone and dialled a number.

Veer was standing by the window camouflaged by the darkness inside his apartment. He observed the bearded man talking on his phone. "Got you," the Captain whispered to himself.

13

Cars, trucks, and trailers passed by in a flash on the six-lane expressway. Narayan drove a navy blue sedan with Saima in the passenger seat for company. The duo was travelling to Agra to meet Narayan's grandfather, Dr. Lalit Sharma.

Saima knitted a white square, which had a small black square in its centre. Her long, slender fingers, arched at an angle, expertly manoeuvring two long needles moving in criss-cross fashion with loose white thread flowing through the needles into a square pattern. Narayan tapped his fingers lightly on the steering wheel in rhythm with the beat of the song playing on his car stereo. It was a Hindi pop-rock song. Vehicles on the grey road travelled backwards in the sedan's rear view mirror. The professor glanced curiously at Saima's knitting.

"It has been a long time since I last saw a woman knit."

Saima raised her eyes from the white square and looked at the professor.

"My mother would knit sweaters for me when I was a kid. They would always fit perfectly. Are you trying to knit a vest?"

"No...not really. Knitting is like meditation for me. It helps me relax."

Saima folded the two needles and placed the square patch on her lap.

"You don't get along with your father, do you?"

Narayan slowly turned towards Saima, "And here I was thinking I would take that secret to my grave," he smiled.

"I am sorry, I do not wish to intrude."

"You did not," Narayan relaxed his shoulders, and had just the right hand on the steering wheel. "My father and I never got along. We were two opposites joined together at the centre because of my mother."

"Like a cream biscuit," Saima commented with a wry smile.

"Correct. Like a cream biscuit," the professor flashed his signature smile. "Two hard biscuits with a soft centre."

Saima laughed out loudly covering her mouth partially with her left hand.

"He thought I was wasting my time studying history. 'Why do you want to study dead people' was a common remark made by my father."

"I have been meaning to ask you...What is it about history that you find interesting? You seem to be a different kind of person when there's an antique or a manuscript around."

"What do you mean...different?"

"Well...how do I say this...," Saima turned in her seat to face Narayan, "You have a certain boyish excitement when it comes to history. You know what I mean? On most occasions you are calm, collected, quiet; but mention a king or an emperor, or a manuscript, or an artefact, and it gets you going like a child riding his shiny new bicycle."

"Hmm, I have never thought about it that way. History is something that I am passionate about. I believe we can learn a lot about our present and future from the past."

"I hear you are an expert on Mughal history. Any particular reason why you chose the Mughals?"

"Miss. Saima Azmi…are you an undercover reporter..?"

"No…why do you ask?"

"You seem to have a list of questions…that's why!" Narayan remarked with a smile.

"I am sorry…I didn't mean to…"

"It's okay…I don't mind answering your questions," the professor adjusted the frame of his spectacles, "Why Mughal history…? The answer's pretty simple. No other dynasty that ruled our land encompassed the savagery and the subtlety that we humans are capable of…as the Mughals did."

Saima listened in rapt attention, her hands clasped together.

"If Babur was a savage warrior set out to establish his dynasty, then Humayun was a connoisseur of the arts, architecture and literature. Akbar, as we all know, ruled with secular principles with an aim to unite Hindus and Muslims, a fair and just ruler who had a penchant for various perspectives on religion. If Jahangir strengthened the economy and focused on the administration during his reign, which brought peace and stability, then Shah Jahan immortalized the Mughal rule in the annals of history with his passion for erecting monuments that captured our collective breath, the Taj Mahal being one of them…"

Narayan paused, his eyes focused on the road ahead. Saima waited for a few seconds.

"Professor...please continue..."

"For a minute I thought I was boring you with the history lesson."

Saima smiled and shook her head.

"With Aurangazeb, the Mughal Empire completed a full circle. Like Babur, he ruthlessly expanded the frontiers of his kingdom to its farthest reaches."

"The Mughals were an interesting people...but what you said just now makes me want to fall in love with them...," Saima could not hide a sense of admiration that she felt for the professor.

"Do you have a girlfriend?"

Narayan was taken by surprise at the rather direct query.

"Why do you ask?"

"It is a little difficult to imagine a smart, handsome, history professor like yourself not having a companion."

"Now you are pulling my leg..."

"Not at all...Any woman would be lucky to have a man who can make a subject like History feel like a wonderful mystery."

"Saima...are you trying to flirt with me...?" the professor asked turning his gaze toward her.

"And if I am...Professor Shastri..."

The professor turned his gaze back to the road with a smile. Narayan had his share of admirers at the university. Every now and then, he received an anonymous note or a letter: girls expressing their adolescent crushes. Narayan took it in his stride and did not pay particular attention to the attention he received. Though Narayan attracted attention from the fairer sex, he never developed a sense of attachment to the women he encountered.

"I must say...I was impressed by the way you held your ground at DIA headquarters. I half expected you to comply with

Captain Veer's directive without complaint. And without your valuable input at Sher-e-Mandal, we would not be on our way to Agra."

"Hmm...," Saima looked out of the car's tinted window, "There was no way I would let that officer...what's his name..."

"Captain Veer," answered Narayan Shastri.

"Yes...Captain Veer. I would never let him dictate terms to me after I had recovered Object No. 27," Saima paused for a few seconds, "It was scary," she turned to face the professor, "when that man attacked me in the hotel room..."

Narayan nodded his head slowly.

Saima continued, "I felt I had a right to know what was going on, what was the big deal about the object."

"There is an air of intrigue that surrounds you, just like history. What you see is not always what you get. I like that in a woman."

"Narayan...I think it is my turn to ask if you are flirting with me?"

The professor smiled, "No, no...not flirting...just telling you what I feel."

"I don't think there is any intrigue or mystery that surrounds me. I was born in Punjab, schooled in Chandigarh, completed a course in Interior Design from Delhi and have been working as a consultant in an interior design agency...you could call me a modern day Mughal moving in and out of the northern states."

Narayan smiled.

"Being the only child, I was pampered a little but my parents never indulged me. Never had boyfriends, but have had my fair share of attention from men. My parents raised me with a lot of freedom, which I never abused..."

From the corner of his eye, Narayan caught Saima's left ear twitch as she spoke. "Wow...sounds like a mini autobiography..."

"Well...you asked for it."

"Indeed I did...I will tell you one thing, though."

Saima nodded her head encouraging the professor to continue.

"It is equally hard to imagine someone like you, blessed with beauty and personality, being single. Now, why would someone like you be unattached?"

Saima's deep brown eyes peered into the distance. She took a couple of seconds to articulate her reply, "I don't think there is a reason why I am single. All I can say is that nobody piqued my interest. Besides, most men I have interacted with seemed to be chauvinists dressed in the garb of modern, freethinking men."

"Hmm...that is an interesting point of view."

"But you...are not like most men I have met. You seem to have a genuine respect for people around you, including women."

Narayan shot a quick glance at Saima.

"Back at Lodi Garden, when you stood up to Captain Veer, I felt safe and sheltered, for the first time in a long time. Not since I left home anyway."

Saima stared at the two long knitting needles and the white square patch between them.

"Narayan...may I ask you something..."

"Sure...go ahead."

"Is it possible that the man who attacked me in the hotel room was Major Salim Khan?"

Narayan thought for a while, "It is a possibility... yes."

"Okay...Have you figured out why the Major would be hunting for the diamond?"

The professor furrowed his brow in concentration and looked at the wide stretch of concrete road being swallowed underneath the hood of the car.

"I have some vague theories...but nothing concrete."

"Let's hear them..."

Narayan drummed his fingers on the steering wheel, deliberating whether to reveal what was on his mind.

"Don't worry professor...your secret's safe with me," Saima ran her thumb and index finger across her lips to imply she was zipping them shut.

"Okay...here goes...Theory number one...Since Major Salim Khan was an integral part of the ISI, he wants to seize the diamond and, probably, take it back to his superiors as a sign of victory against India. Our loss would be their gain...somewhat like a pseudo-battle."

"Hmm...hmm....," Saima rubbed her chin and nodded her head.

"The second theory...and my favourite one...is that Major Khan is not working on his own. He has, in fact, been hired by a person who belongs to the bloodline of the great Mughals. The world does not know the identity of this person or that he/she is a descendant. When this person gets the diamond back, they would have reclaimed a lost glory of their famed ancestors...so to say."

"Not bad...I know why this is your favourite theory...because it involves bloodlines and, most importantly, Mughals. I can imagine you salivating over such a prospect. Right...professor?"

"Yes...Saima...," Narayan had a wide smile plastered on his face. "Theory number three..."

"Yes, please..."

"Major Salim Khan is...," Narayan paused.

Saima looked at him, "Is...what?"

"Major Salim Khan is an alien..."

Saima raised her eyebrows.

"Major Salim Khan is an alien in the guise of a human being who has travelled to planet earth in search of a magical stone. Once he lays his hand on the stone, he will be crowned emperor of his planet..."

Narayan looked at Saima with a straight face.

"Ha ha...hahaha...," Saima's visage broke into peals of laughter. Her shoulders sashayed as she laughed; a part of her mouth was covered with her left hand.

"Too good...professor...theory number three is my favourite," Saima said between fits of laughter.

The professor adjusted the frame of his spectacles and steadied his hands on the wheel.

Saima leaned back in her seat, a smile lingered on her face.

"What do you think could be a possible connection between the diamond and Major Khan?" the professor asked Saima.

Saima pursed her lips, "Well...I think he is searching for the diamond to satiate his own greed. The Major's probably looking to make millions, if not billions, by trading the diamond once he gets his hands on it."

"Hmm...yes...it could be plain greed, a most fundamental, yet harmful human sentiment."

Narayan eyed a food court on the expressway, a few metres away. "Would it be ok if we stopped for a coffee?"

"That would be perfect!"

The blue sedan glided to the exit for the food court.

In the distance, a black sedan broke across the horizon and sped in a straight line. Inside the sedan, Major Khan stared at his cell phone screen; it read 'Stopping at food court'.

14

It was late at night when the navy blue sedan entered the compound of Dr. Lalit Sharma.The professor and Saima alighted from the car parked a few feet away from the house along the driveway. Behind them, the servant, dressed in a warm winter jacket and monkey cap closed the white iron gate of the compound, sliding it shut. The noise made by the gate sliding shut woke up a couple of stray dogs that howled for a minute or two. Dr. Lalit Sharma stayed in a single-storied row house. Plots to the left and right of the house were vacant. A stiff, cold breeze blew across the compound; Saima instinctively clutched her arms together to keep warm. The servant trotted towards the duo; he greeted the two and informed them that the doctor had gone out of town to survey an archaeological site and would return the next morning.

Narayan, Saima, and the servant entered the living room, the professor had a duffle bag and Saima carried a backpack.The room was simple, devoid of any embellishment or decor. A sofa set occupied the far right of the room, a dining table sat a few feet away from the sofa set. Saima relaxed with the comfortable warmth that filled the room, stark opposite to the cold outdoor weather. The servant collected the duffle bag and backpack, enquiring whether dinner should be served. Narayan and Saima politely refused and requested to be shown to their respective rooms. With the duffle bag in one hand and the backpack in another, the servant led the way.

Saima kept her black backpack on top of the bed and unzipped it. She removed a lavender-coloured cotton tracksuit and placed it on the side of the backpack. Slipping out of her jacket, she unzipped her jeans and let it slide to the floor, stepping out of them. Straightening her left arm, she pulled out the full sleeve top, folded it and placed it inside the backpack. A mirror held Saima's reflection draped in red thermal wear hugging her figure, which stood out in stark contrast to the washed out colours of the room. Her hair, straight and smooth, sashayed across her back as she removed her hairpins and placed them on a dressing table next to the bed. She ran her fingers across the scalp and tied her hair in a loose single knot. Saima picked out a square-shaped cream container from her backpack. She flipped open the lid, dipped her fingers into the cream, twirled her fingers to scoop a portion of the cream, and applied it on her face and neck massaging it in circular motion. Unclipping her square black earrings, she placed them carefully next to the hairpins. She quickly slipped into her lavender tracksuit, picked the pair of jeans from the floor and kept it at the foot of her bed. Saima rubbed her palms together and slid under the blanket, placing her head on the pillow. Her eyelids drooped shut, her mind wandered.

Her mind wandered to the conversation she had with the professor on her road trip to Agra. If she had been any younger, she may have given in to the initial heady rush of attraction. *But you are a big girl now...*she reminded herself, half asleep half awake; *and big girls don't fall in love with men they have known for just a couple of days.* There was something about Narayan that drew her to him. Maybe it was his calm demeanour, maybe it was his superior knowledge of his field of choice. For the first time in her life, Saima felt a strong urge to envelop herself around a man and stay like that for the rest of the time. She clasped her palms and placed it between her thighs. Sleep embraced Saima as her mind wandered again.

The pendulum of a wall clock swung left right left right. Narayan turned over in his bed. His eyes were calm, closed, ready to fall asleep; but a restless mind prodded him, kept him awake. For the first time in his life, he wanted to continue his conversation with a woman for the rest of the time. If anyone asked him about his ideal woman, Saima would be it: an intoxicating mix of character and beauty. The professor felt himself drown in Saima's deep brown eyes. *Narayan…you better show some restraint…at least till we find the diamond….*the professor reminded himself. The pendulum swung back and forth.

"Narayan! Good Morning…boy! Great to see you…!"

The portly figure of Dr. Lalit Sharma strode into the living hall, where Narayan was having his morning coffee at the dining table. Dr. Sharma hugged Narayan and patted his back. "It has been a long time…how is the world famous history professor doing?"

Narayan replied, slightly embarrassed, "Not world famous or anything nanu…"

"You know I just about told everyone I know about how you turned down an offer to teach at Princeton and decided to stay back and contribute to the betterment of students here. They are all so proud of you," Dr. Sharma placed his hand gently on Narayan's right cheek, "And so am I."

The professor smiled, feeling a rare sense of accomplishment.

"So...tell me...what brings you to the house of a withering, old man..."

"Nanu...you are not old. In fact, you can still give guys my age a run for their money."

"Boy...do not butter me...I know it is an old habit of yours..."

Narayan smiled, "How was your trip?"

"Good...ok...not bad...A real estate developer came upon an archaeological find while digging the land. I was called in to assess the worth of the find."

"What about the land and its development?"

"The developer, a nice chap, has offered to hand over the land to ASI in return for a plot in the vicinity."

"That's very generous of him," Narayan commented.

"Yes...indeed it is. Tell me Narayan, is there anything I can help you with?"

A faint sound of anklets rustling echoed in the background. Dr. Lalit Sharma turned back for a second and then faced his grandson again. He looked at Narayan with a quizzical expression on his face.

"Narayan...did you marry?"

"Nanu..!No...I did not..."

"Girlfirend...then?"

Narayan Shastri shook his head.

The rustling anklets grew louder; Saima entered the living room.

Dr. Lalit Sharma looked at Saima and smiled, "Hi. I am Dr. Lalit Sharma. And you must be..."

"Saima Azmi..."

Dr. Sharma shook her hand warmly. "Now I am intrigued... you must tell me what has brought the two of you here...but first...Saima what will you have?"

"Coffee...if it would not be too much trouble," replied Saima courteously.

"It's no trouble at all...Birju..."

The servant appeared with two coffee cups on a tray and placed it on the dining table. Saima and Dr. Sharma took their seats at the table along with Narayan.

"Nanu, it is a long story..."

Dr. Sharma sipped on his coffee. "I have all the time in the world."

Narayan Shastri began, "It is about a diamond bigger than the Koh-i-Noor and Darya-e-Noor..."

Minutes ticked away on a wall clock.

Dr. Lalit Sharma glanced at his empty cup of coffee, and then looked at Narayan. Dr. Sharma tapped his finger on the table in rhythmic manner. He got up from the table, "I think I have just the thing for you. Be back in a jiffy. Saima, another cup of coffee?"

"I'm fine, thank you," Saima replied, once again in a courteous manner.

Dr. Sharma walked out of the living room. Saima sat on her chair, legs crossed, with her right elbow resting on the table and her chin resting on the elbow.

"Did you sleep well?" Narayan adjusted the frame of his spectacles and looked at Saima.

She sat up erect and replied, "Yes. How about you?"

"Yeah...good...listen...am sorry about earlier...," Narayan spoke in a soft tone.

Saima leaned closer, "What for?"

"Nanu...I hope he did not make you feel uncomfortable."

Saima shook her head, gesturing 'no'.

"The thing is...he has never seen me with a girl before. That is why he was a little excited when he saw you. I hope you don't think I suggested to him that there was something going between us..."

"Narayan...relax...I didn't mind it all." Saima replied with a gentle smile spreading across her face.

"Okay...," Narayan averted his gaze to the empty sofa set. "Saima," the professor paused. He ruminated whether should confess what he felt yesterday night. Narayan was about to say something when his grandfather walked in.

"I'm back," Dr. Sharma walked to the table carrying a black laptop with him. He placed the laptop on the table equidistant from Narayan and Saima, and took a seat between them. The three of them formed a triumvirate with the laptop being the focal point. The laptop was in mint-fresh condition without as much of a scratch or a mark on its surface.

"This laptop...," Lalit Sharma began, "is password protected. If you want me to type in the password and give you access... Narayan...you will have to answer a pop quiz. Saima," he turned to face her, "you can help out your partner as well."

"Nanu..." the professor pleaded.

"Boy...this is for not visiting your Nanu more often. Now, I understand the gravity of your situation. The quiz is a short one and based on my grandson's area of expertise, the Mughals... okay...are we ready?" Lalit Sharma looked at his grandson and Saima Azmi. Both nodded their heads.

"Right...first question coming up...What is the name of one of the largest diamonds known to us...which is now a part of the crown jewels..."

"The Koh-i-Noor," answered Narayan instantly.

"Correct," Lalit Sharma opened the screen of the laptop.

"Next question...The prince who led an uprising against his father, an emperor. The prince still became emperor when his father passed away. Who is this prince?"

"Jahangir. Next question please..."

Dr. Sharma smiled and pressed the power button located below the screen. The laptop tuned on. "Okay...the symbol of love built by Shah Jahan in memory of his wife, also the name of a popular tea brand..."

The professor looked at Saima.

"Taj Mahal," she replied.

"Well done, Saima," Dr. Sharma nodded. "Next question... Who was the last Mughal emperor?"

"Bahadur Shah Zafar..."

Lalit Sharma looked at his grandson with a serious expression. "Are you sure? Confident? Should I lock the answer?" He imitated the mannerism of the superstar who hosted the Indian version of 'Who wants to be a millionaire'.

"Yes please...," Narayan replied, almost pleading.

With the password keyed in, the screen flickered to display the start menu. "Narayan...this laptop contains images of a vast number of paintings, relics, and manuscripts which are all related to the Mughal period. It may not be an exaggeration to say that the entire Mughal dynasty is in this laptop," Dr. Sharma smiled. "This laptop belonged to your mother. She collected these images on a whim. Spent a better part of ten years doing it. Come to think of it, maybe it was a mother's intuition telling her that these images would help her son out one day." Dr. Sharma got up from the table, "Narayan...can you guess what the password was?"

Narayan Shastri rubbed his chin and replied, "Her name..."

The grandfather smiled, "I need to go to the office for a while. You kids peruse the images and sort it out. I will meet you in the evening. Birju...."

The servant arrived and cleared the coffee cups from the table. Dr. Sharma exited the living room. Narayan and Saima moved to the sofa set with the laptop.

The professor tapped his index finger twice in quick succession on the mouse pad of the laptop to open the lone folder, which sat on the start screen. Narayan clicked on the very first image of the folder: a woman facing the mirror with a string of white pearls in her hand, a white robe draping her neck; the woman eyed the pearl with a sort of excitement women express while wearing a piece of jewellery for the first time. Her eyebrows raised half in anticipation, a smile beginning to form on her pink lips.

"Without doubt, this laptop belongs to my mother," Narayan Shastri commented looking at the image of the woman in the painting which had magnified to fit the screen.

Saima looked at the image. "Does she remind you of your mother?"

"In a way, yes," Narayan pointed to the pearls in the image, "My mother owned a pearl set. Every day, in the morning, she would wear her pearls before leaving the house. It was a ritual for her, a kind of morning prayer."

"I am sure she must have been a very beautiful woman."

Narayan and Saima began scanning through the images in the folder, one after the other: paintings of kings on conquests; kings holding courts; queens posing before mirrors; queens posing before kings, expressing beautiful smiles and seductive glances; manuscripts inked in beautiful calligraphy; ancient structures; and antiquated relics flashed on the screen.

A woman knelt beside a tomb, covered in black, with her eyes lowered. An aura of sadness enveloped the woman, sadness which was reminiscent of beauty rather than tragedy. This image reflected on the professor's spectacles. He stared at the image for a while. As the image of the woman at the tomb began to fade out, Narayan paused the slideshow. The professor went back a couple of images to bring up a mural portrait of Shah Jahan. His eyes glanced over the portrait. The next image professor Shastri brought on screen was that of the Taj Mahal. With quick touches, Narayan placed the three images on the screen one after the other. Saima looked at the three images and then at the professor.

"Saima, would you like to listen to a story..."

The Diamond - II

A father[8] sat beside the bed of his daughter, anxious about her failing health. The daughter[9] lay motionless in bed, covered in a woollen blanket. Her face pale, drops of sweat formed on her brow. The soft cushion of the bed hardly registered the presence of the daughter. Her body – light, almost lifeless – seemed to be floating on a thin layer of air above the bed. Brown prayer beads slipped through the slender, ageing fingers of the father, who prayed silently. Beneath the blanket lay a body, scarred with

---

[8] Shah Jahan

[9] Jahanara Begum

burnt flesh, trying to heal. A slender, almost imperceptible, breath flowed in and out of her fragile body, keeping her alive. The father, palms close to his face, back bent, was not sure whether it was an accident or an intentional attempt to murder his daughter. Her evening robe was sprayed with perfume oils and placed on the bed. The clothes caught fire, which raged through the room engulfing the daughter in its wicked flames. As the sun set below the horizon, her clothes set ablaze in a bright yellow fire; the body, burning bright, swayed to and fro like a wick alight. It was a while before the daughter's maids rushed to her aid and doused the fire.

The father thought it a minor miracle that her face was left untouched by the fire. Herbal extracts were applied to the scars on the body, potions mixed together and fed by the resident physician of the palace. Nothing seemed to alleviate her pain.

He checked on her, the breathing had stopped, the body lay motionless.

There was only one recourse left now. A bright, shining diamond was brought forth. The father closed his eyes and whispered a silent prayer to the diamond: calling on a mystical power that had blessed his dynasty to heal his daughter, and bring her breath back. He placed the tip of the diamond on her forehead. The only sound in the room was of his heartbeat, beating hard. The daughter began to breathe again, her breath was soft and slow; she slowly opens her eyes. The father breathed a sigh of relief and thanked the Almighty. He could not afford to lose the last living memory of his beloved wife.[10]

---

[10] Mumtaz Mahal

The new emperor sat tall on his throne, running his hands over the gold plated armrest. Aurangzeb's destiny was written the day Shah Jahan declared Dara Shikoh to be his successor. The third son of Shah Jahan believed that he possessed the administrative wherewithal and military prowess to be crowned the next Mughal Emperor after Shah Jahan. He felt Darah Sikoh was being favoured only because he was the eldest among his brothers, and his father's favourite son. Darah Sikoh did not possess the necessary military and administrative acumen to be a Mughal emperor. Aurangzeb would fight for his right to be crowned emperor; even if it meant fighting a war with his own brother. After all, power struggles had been a regular feature of his family: sons fighting fathers, brother battling brother. The new emperor, too, would have been the victim of a family feud.

Shah Jahan had invited Aurangzeb to his palace in order to resolve the battle for succession that was raging between Darah Sikoh and Aurangzeb. The third son readied his convoy, and was about to set out to his father's palace when he received a messenger from his younger sister[11]. The messenger alerted Aurangzeb about a plot hatched by Shah Jahan and Darah Sikoh to kill him when he reached the palace. The emperor viewed his third son as a threat to his throne and wanted him eliminated.

Aurangzeb did not make the trip.

He bided his time. Aurangzeb waited for an opportunity to engage his eldest brother and take over the throne. It was the only thing he wanted, it was the only thing that would satiate him.

Shah Jahan fell ill. With the emperor incapacitated, Darah Sikoh stepped into his father's throne. What the eldest son did

[11] Roshanara Begum

not realize that his brothers would see his act as manipulating the situation to his advantage. No one wanted to play second fiddle, everyone wanted to be an emperor.

Shah Jahan was recuperating under the watchful care of Darah Sikoh; however, like white smoke which dissipates from a candlewick that has been put out, rumours of the emperor's death dissipated throughout the kingdom. Shah Shuja, who was Viceroy of Bengal, and Murad Baksh, the Viceroy of Gujarat – brothers of Darah Sikoh, sons of the Shah Jahan – believed their elder brother was hiding the death of their father to assume the throne and be crowned the new emperor. The Viceroy of Bengal and the Viceroy of Gujarat claimed their independence and marched on to Agra to challenge the throne.

This was the opportunity Aurangzeb was waiting for.

Shah Jahan had partially recovered his health. Darah Sikoh urged the emperor to send two batches of his imperial army to halt the march of Shah Shuja and Murad Baksh. The emperor complied.

Shah Shuja's army was routed in Benaras. The second Imperial army, which had set out to thwart Murad Baksh's progress found themselves facing not one but two armies: that of Murad Baksh and Aurangzeb.

The third son had joined forces with his brother to defeat the Imperial army. Victory was theirs. The two armies continued their march to the throne.

Aurangzeb clashed with Darah Sikoh at the Battle of Samugarh. The well-disciplined and battle-hardened army of the former easily crushed the disconnected and hastily put together army of the latter. The throne was just a hand's reach away from the third son.

After the victory, Aurangzeb's reputation rose as a brilliant military strategist and a feared leader. He used his reputation cleverly to order the execution of his ally and brother, Murad Baksh for the murder of a divan of Gujarat.

Before joining forces, the two brothers had decided to partition the empire between them once they ascended the throne. It was never Aurangzeb's intention to share the throne with anyone.

The new emperor sat on his throne and looked at his courtyard which was empty at the present moment. This would be the seat from where he would rule his kingdom. But first, he had to take care of a family matter: order the cold blooded execution of his eldest brother.

It was Roshanara who insisted that Aurangzeb eliminate all trace of the enemy before they posed a threat to his rule. The new emperor, already indebted to his younger sister for warning him about his father's plot to kill him, did not have any reason to turn down his sister. If Dara Shikoh were to be eliminated, Aurangzeb would not face any threat to his throne, at least from his own family. The elimination of the eldest son would also tell his father that the new emperor was now in command.

Shah Jahan sat at his dining table after offering his evening prayers. Far removed from the grandeur associated with an emperor's meal, he looked at the dry, cracking rotis and cold dal curry served on his plate. The room holding Shah Jahan reflected his sense of despair, pulling the man deeper and deeper into its suffocating bosom. All hope had drained away from his eyes. An oddly shaped turban, coloured gold placed at a corner on the table caught his eye. It stood silent, almost dead. A fly traced its path to and positioned itself on the turban. It moved around the turban with eager anticipation, as if it had found its evening meal. Shah Jahan was intrigued, but, at the same time, a sense of fear washed over him. It was never a good sign when a fly settled itself on anything, let alone a turban. The father got up and moved slowly, taking one step at a time, his feet weighed down by age and passing time. Wrinkled fingers untied the rope tied around the top of the gold turban. The nose instinctively sensed a foreboding stench. As the turban fell away on the table revealing its content, an intense sense of grief and sorrow flashed across his eyes. The rush of emotion was so intense that Shah Jahan felt his world go blank as his world collapsed around him. A father collapsed to the ground.

What the bag revealed, was a neatly sliced head of Darah Sikoh: Shah Jahan's eldest son, the son who was his father's favourite.

Roshanara Begum sat up on her bed, propped with plush satin pillows. A white negligee draped the firm, slender curves outlining her body. The bed was covered on all sides with transparent silk curtains, with partitions to allow the cool breeze streaming through the open window of the bedroom. Roshanara Begum leaned back with a satisfied expression playing on her lips. The new emperor, Aurangzeb, had crowned his younger sister as the Imperial Princess. Basking in the afterglow of her new title, she had ordered the public beheading of Darah Sikoh, who she feared could not only threaten Aurangzeb's rule, but could eliminate his younger sister as well if he came to power. The new emperor let Roshanara have her way and that pleased her.

Darah Sikoh was paraded around the streets like a common thief, bound in chains, dragged like a stray dog from corner to corner before being led to the executioner. Bystanders were witnessing the first instance of the power that Roshanara would come to wield during Aurangzeb's reign. The executioner flexed his shoulders and arms and brought the heavy sword, with precision, on the tender neck muscles of the eldest son of Shah Jahan. His head popped out gently off his body and fell down on the ground, rolling before it came to rest. Blood from the decapitated man's neck splattered like drizzling rain on bystanders: a woman fainted, which seemed to commemorate the first public beheading of the new emperor's reign.

Roshanara Begum now closed her eyes, her lips quivering with pleasure as the head of a young man bobbed up and down between her thighs. The new Imperial Princess derived pleasure not only from the efforts of the young man positioned between her legs, but also from imagining the beheading of her eldest brother, which filled her with the most powerful aphrodisiac known to humankind: power.

The newly appointed Imperial Princess was also pleased about the fact that she had replaced Jahanara.

Roshanara had had always been jealous of her elder sister and the eldest of Shah Jahan's children. Jahanara was always the apple of her father's eye and received his undivided love and attention. The younger sister felt she was treated like a pariah, like a bastard child, when compared to her elder sister. The favouritism filled Roshanara Begum with envy and hatred.

Tonight, she felt happy; she felt a measure of peace after having upstaged her elder sister: Jahanara Begum, everyone's favourite.

Beads of sweat rolled off the back of the young man as he rose above her legs. His hips then descended to conduct its final act. Roshanara grasped his young, tender flesh and closed her eyes.

Jahanara could not believe that the dilapidated figure lying before her was once an emperor, a ruler who commanded the loyalty of a million people across the Indian subcontinent. Her father, Shah Jahan was now a pale, dissipated figure: the cruel beheading of his eldest son had taken its toll. The man who was once emperor, lay still on his bed, life ebbing away from his soul with each passing minute. The chamber he rested in echoed the fast deteriorating health of Shah Jahan. Everything stood still. Gossamer drapes covering the windows did not move an inch. Even the yellow flames from candlesticks stood straight and tall from their respective wicks encased in blue-coloured chandeliers. Shadows in the room lengthened as the soft yellow halo emanating from candles grew brighter. Jahanara kept her hand on her father's hand which lay stretched out by his side. She closed her eyes and uttered a silent prayer. The daughter willed with every inch of her being that her father get back his past glory. Every inch of Shah Jahan's being, however, was willing him towards the final light.

The daughter knew her father was not perfect. He was always partial towards Jahanara and Darah; Aurangzeb and Roshanara were left behind in their shadows. As a kid, Jahanara had always questioned her father's partiality, which Shah Jahan brushed aside as the naivete of a child. When the boys became men and the girls blossomed into fine young women, the emperor's favouritism became the catalyst for the battle of his throne. Shah Jahan made Jahanara the Imperial Princess; the decision did not meet any resistance. When the emperor proclaimed Darah Sikoh to be the next Mughal Emperor, the decision triggered a bloody family feud. Aurangzeb defied his father's order and challenged his elder brother for the throne. The eldest daughter, as was her habit, picked the side of her father and elder brother. Shah Jahan realized that as long as his third son was alive, his favourite son would not have an easy road ahead. The emperor concocted a devious plan. He would invite Aurangzeb over to the palace on the pretext of discussing the matter of who would be the next emperor. Once Aurangzeb set foot in the palace, the upstart would be captured and then killed. Shah Jahan discussed his plan with Darah Sikoh. Unbeknown to father and son, Roshanara overheard the plot to kill her brother. After weighing the gravity of the situation, she decided to warn Aurangzeb and forbid him from accepting her father's invitation. A messenger was sent to Aurangzeb in the thick of night.

When his third son did not arrive to the palace, Shah Jahan knew his plan had failed. He now feared for his future and that of his eldest son. Aurangzeb was, after all, his own offspring. If the father could think of killing his son because he was a threat to the throne, the son too would be capable of it.

Jahanara kept her right hand on her father's emaciated forehead. Her touch was as light as a feather.

Aurangzeb was emperor now and had placed Shah Jahan under house arrest and exiled him away from the seat of power so that he could not interfere. The new emperor overruled his father's order and made Roshanara Begum the Imperial Princess. Jahanara did not care whether she had a title or a palace of her own, all that she cared for was her father. The daughter brought forth the diamond and placed it on her father's forehead. She remembered how her father had willed the diamond to bring his daughter back from the dead; she prayed that the diamond work its miracle one more time. Everything stood absolutely still in the room.

The emperor rubbed his furrowed brow. It was not the first time the hedonistic indulgences of the Imperial Princess had reached his ears. On the one hand, he coerced his religious ways on his subjects; on the other hand, his sister carelessly and conveniently flouted his strict religious discipline. Aurangzeb felt he could no longer control Roshanara. He dedicatedly followed the ways of his religion; sometimes to the extreme that it began to alienate his own subjects who believed in a different religion. The attempts of earlier secular Mughal Emperors seemed wasted. While Aurangzeb's predecessors tried to unite their polity, his steadfast and dogmatic rule divided them.

This was, primarily, the reason why he was now frustrated with Roshanara Begum. He had heard enough about her greed – the Imperial Princess amassed land and gold at her will and whimsy; she misused the powers Aurnangzeb had bestowed on her in good faith before he left for a long and arduous military campaign in the Deccan Plateau. There was nothing Roshanara Begum wouldn't do to increase her financial gains. Greed was something Aurangzeb was strictly against, because it was abhorred in the religious doctrines on which he conducted himself. Being an Imperial Princess, it was a Mughal tradition that Roshanara Begum abstain from any form of physical intimacy. However, her insatiable lust for gold was only equalled by her unquenchable desire for a hedonistic lifestyle. She led a bohemian life, having multiple sexual partners, some out in the open, others behind closed doors.

What worried Aurangzeb the most were the rumours that he could not discipline his own sister. She had imposed her iron-fisted rule on the emperor's harem, which was not taken kindly by his wives. *An emperor who cannot govern his kingdom is not fit to be a ruler, but an emperor who cannot control the actions of his own sibling has no right to be a ruler...*mused Aurangzeb. He was in a fix. He did not know what to do with Roshanara. She was his sister, but had come to mean much more to him. Whenever he felt world-weary and troubled, he found solace in the warm embrace of Roshanara Begum.

The emperor sat on his throne. Empty seats of the courtyard stared back at him. On the walls adjacent to the throne hung paintings of maulanas reading religious texts to people, conducting rituals, and praying. Aurangzeb liked to sit on his throne, a seat of power, and clear his mind when he did not have clarity of thought. This night was one such instance when the emperor was not sure about the path he needed to take. He had already banished Roshanara from his court, stripped her of her title, and ordered her to remain in seclusion and live a pious life in her garden palace. The emperor's messenger had just informed him that his sister, despite his stern warning, had been found in the arms of another male companion at her garden palace. This infuriated the devout Mughal Emperor.

Aurangzeb deliberated. It was then it struck him that Roshanara, by refusing to mend her ways in spite of repeated pardons, had insulted and abused her position as the emperor's sister. In her actions, the emperor saw a lack of respect for his way of life, which implied a lack of respect of the emperor as well. The brother had done everything he could for his sister; but Roshanara did not seem to appreciate Aurangzeb's gestures. Something had to be done.

On a still, sultry night, the sister who was once Imperial Princess sat on her bed with her head drooped between her shoulders. Roshanara felt a numbness creeping over her body, which started from her toes and made its way to her fingers. Dressed in a black negligee, her pale, fair skin provided a striking contrast. She looked at herself in a mirror placed opposite the bed. What was once firm, slender flesh had now transformed into wrinkled, fat deposits: the hands of time had left its inevitable marks. She tilted her body and rested her head gently on a satin red pillow. Roshanara could feel the warmth and slow breathing of another being lying next to her; however, her mind could neither identify nor recognize the person. The sister, who was once Imperial Princess, doubted whether this was a dream. She had been the centre of the emperor's universe. Could it be possible that she was now banished to the outer fringes. Roshanara closed her eyes; her mind flowed with memories: of a childhood spent waiting for her father to shower his love on her, of Aurangzeb offering her the entire world on a platter, of her trying to find love as she took on one lover after another, of her brother exiling her because of her unbridled greed. Roshanara opened her eyes; this was not a dream. Her eyes darted to a gold challis kept on the windowsill at the head of the bed. The faint impression of her lips was etched on the mouth of the cup. The numbness spread to her eyes. Her eyes closed for one last time.

Roshanara and her lover were found dead at her garden palace.

In an ironic twist of fate, the emperor had the body of his sister interred at Roshanara Bagh: a garden she had designed and commissioned herself. Rumour was rife it was the emperor who had poisoned his dear sister. The men and women close to

Aurangzeb knew that he would never bring himself to do it. It seemed Roshanara had decided to take her own life in the end.

With Roshanara's body slowly decaying in her tomb, Jahanara's influence on Aurangzeb grew slowly and steadily, like the warmth of spring after a harsh winter. Aurangzeb always needed an elder woman in whom he could confide and Jahanara, with her disciplined way of life, was the perfect choice.

There was a time when the emperor and his eldest sister did not see eye to eye. Aurangzeb could not bring himself to forgive her for supporting her father and Dara Shikoh during the conflict for the throne's succession. It was Jahanara's undying loyalty to Shah Jahan and the willingness to give everything up to take care of her ailing father, which impressed Aurangzeb. She imposed self-exile for eight years to be alongside Shah Jahan during his house arrest at Agra Fort.

When Shah Jahan passed away, Aurangzeb reconciled with Jahanara. The reconciliation led to the emperor bestowing the title 'Empress of Princesses' on Jahanara. By then, Roshanara had lost favour with her brother due to her carefree and libertine attitude. With time, the emperor's respect for Jahanara grew to reverence. There was no one else, besides Jahanara, who could hold a discussion with Aurangzeb and argue about his strict regulation of public life in accordance with his conservative religious beliefs. She would occasionally chide her younger brother but never interfered in the way Aurangzeb ruled his empire.

The emperor used her valuable inputs, but did not shift from his conservative ways.

A white marble tomb, intricate in its design, rested in silence. Chirpings of birds echoed in the background as leaves rustled in a gentle breeze. Beside the white tomb sat a figure draped in black. Shah Jahan had passed away; the intricately designed vault, his final resting place. Yet, Jahanara had not forgotten about the bond that existed between father and daughter.

The daughter had wanted a state funeral for her beloved father. Eminent nobles would carry his body, wrapped in a ceremonial robe, to his grave. A procession of notable citizens and officials would follow; they would scatter silver coins to the poor and needy.

The emperor refused such an ostentatious farewell for a father who had tried to kill him. Besides, his dogmatic principles did not allow such a grand funeral. Shah Jahan's body would be washed in accordance with Islamic rites, then taken by river in a sandalwood coffin to its final resting place.

There was one luxury that Aurangzeb afforded Jahanara. His father's final remains would be interred next to the one person that Shah Jahan loved and treasured the most – his wife, Mumtaz Mahal.

Jahanara placed her hand on the head of the tomb, as if reassuring her father's spirit that she was still here and would never leave his side. Her eyes glanced at a spot near the centre of tomb. A certain aura shone through that particular spot. She had given back everything she received from her father…

Saima's gaze was fixed on the lady in black sitting next to the white tomb. She found herself to be transfixed by the image.

"Well…what do you think?"

Narayan's voice drew Saima out of the image. She looked at the professor, and tried to connect her train of thought.

"Saima...do you think Jahanara could hold our next clue to the diamond?"

Saima looked at the image once again. The effect the image had on her slowly ebbed. "It is a possibility..."

15

Dressed in a white kurta pyjama topped with a black sleeveless khadi jacket, the retired ASI director appeared fresh and bright. Dr. Sharma tilted the bottle to a precise angle and carefully poured the liquid content of the bottle into a dry, empty glass. He looked at Saima, "What will the lady have?"

"What the men are having."

"That's my girl," Dr. Sharma tilted the bottle over Saima's empty glass.

Three glasses stood on the table with equal amounts of reddish brown whisky. A plate of potato crisps was placed at the centre of the table. Sounds of knife chopping on a wooden board and hot oil frying its contents inside a pan gently echoed across the living room. A room heater hummed from a corner.

"Cheers!" Dr. Sharma raised his glass, "To my grandson, the best history professor in the world."

Narayan shook his head, smiling, "Cheers," The professor took a sip from his glass.

"Is this single malt?" Saima enquired taking her first sip.

"Yes...it is. You sure do know your whiskey, young lady."

"Thanks to my roommate in college," Saima quipped.

"Saima...ever since Narayan turned 20, I would invite him over once or twice a year, pour him a drink, and interrogate him."

"Interrogate him?"

"Yes. I would put the spotlight on him and ask him if he had any girlfriends, if he fancied anyone, if he had any crushes," Dr. Sharma took a second sip. "But my boy here was as straight as an arrow," he placed his hand on Narayan's hand. "It is good to see him in the company of a woman..."

"Nanu...it is not like that..." Narayan offered a weak explanation.

"What's not like that...Saima is a fine, young woman..."

"Nanu please stop," Narayan implored, "You are embarrassing her."

"Am I...," Dr. Sharma turned his attention to Saima. "Dear... am I embarrassing you?"

Saima half smiled, half blushed, and quickly took a sip of her whiskey.

"Okay...I get the message...let's change the topic. Did you kids make any headway with the diamond case?"

The professor looked at Saima, "Well...we figure that Jahanara, the eldest child of Shah Jahan received the diamond from her father. Whether she passed on the diamond to Aurangzeb or kept it for herself...we don't know for sure as yet. The trail goes cold from Jahanara...but she is our next clue."

"Maybe if we find out more about Jahanara, it will lead us to Noor-e-jahan," chipped in Saima.

Dr. Sharma bit into a potato crisp and munched in rhythmic manner. "I don't think the diamond reached Aurangzeb," stated Shastri's grandfather with a certain amount of belief.

Narayan and Saima looked at the septuagenarian.

"Nanu...is this a fact or something you have inferred?"

"It is something I have inferred and I will tell you why," Dr. Sharma took a sip from his glass, "Aurangzeb was a complex character. He led a strict, disciplined life dedicated to the ways of his religion. The sense of discipline in his character gave him an aura to rule over the empire. However, history will probably remember him as a divisive figure: an emperor who was so blinded by his religious belief that he had no qualms in enforcing it on his subjects. This led to his people being divided on religious lines."

Narayan and Saima listened attentively to Dr. Sharma while munching on potato crisps.

"Though Aurangzeb is considered a religious oppressor, one must not forget that he also made the Mughal Empire the richest it had ever been. Unlike his predecessors, Aurangzeb did not indulge in extravagances like constructing monuments of splendour. It is said that the man made copies of the Quran to generate revenue for his personal expense and never dipped his hands into the funds of the royal treasury," Dr. Sharma took a large sip of whisky and continued, "The reason why I feel the diamond may not have reached his hands is simple...Aurangzeb, being the devout Muslim that he was, would not have believed in some stone carrying a blessing that would forward his dynasty. For him, destiny lay in the hands of the almighty and no force on earth could change it."

Dr. Sharma reached out for a potato crisp and bit into it, munching slowly. "I believe even if the diamond was given to Aurangzeb, he would have smirked and brushed it aside."

"Interesting...very interesting...," remarked Saima.

Birju walked into the living room carrying grilled cottage cheese on a large, white ceramic plate to the table. He placed the plate on the table and walked back to the kitchen. The reddish-brown coating of the cottage cheese bore resemblance to the whisky in the three glasses.

"Looks appetizing," commented Narayan.

"Birju is a good cook. I am sure he will not disappoint. What are you waiting for...dig in," Dr. Sharma trapped a piece of cottage cheese between his index and ring fingers of his right hand and brought it to his mouth. Saima and Narayan reached out for a piece at the same time. Their fingers brushed at the tips, the two withdrew their fingers from the plate simultaneously.

"Please...go ahead," Narayan said withdrawing his fingers to his glass.

"It's okay...you go ahead...," replied Saima with a smile.

"Oh! You two are priceless. Here, you take one, and you take one...," the septuagenarian gave a piece of grilled cheese to Saima and his grandson respectively. "Now eat."

Saima took a slow bite off the cottage cheese, her lips closing on the tender piece. "Mmm...this is delicious...," her fingers held the grilled piece.

"I told you...," Dr. Sharma turned to face his grandson. "Talking of Aurangzeb, how is the bull-headed obstinate father of yours doing?"

Narayan bit into the cottage cheese and took a swig of whisky to wash it down. "Dad's doing all right. We met him before coming down to Agra. In fact, he was the one who suggested we talk to you."

"That's very generous of my son-in-law."

"I feel he's a changed man. Age has probably softened him a bit."

"My boy…if you tell me that Aurangzeb was a secular ruler, I will believe you. But I cannot believe that Lieutenant General Madan Shastri can change. Ever."

Saima took a sip of her whisky and listened keenly to the exchange between grandfather and grandson with her elbow resting on the table.

"Nanu… I am telling you…there is something different about him. When I met him, he told me that he wanted the two of us to have a conversation and sort things out."

"Hmmm…that is out of character for your father," Dr. Sharma tapped his fingers on the table as if trying to drum up a thought he had forgotten. "One thing I have still not understood after all these years," he took a sip finishing his drink, "is why your mother, may her soul rest in peace, chose a strict stubborn disciplinarian to spend the rest of her life with. I could have got her the best Brahmin boy who would have kept her like a queen… I had warned her, I told her that he will convert you into an inmate of his prison. Do you know what you mother's reply was?"

Narayan shook his head.

"She said she would rather stay imprisoned with him than have her freedom with another man," the septuagenarian shook his head with his palms on the forehead. "She was such a carefree spirit."

The professor stared at his glass. It served as a mirror for looking into his childhood memories. Though his father was a stern man, Narayan could not recollect him ever being harsh with his mother. She had a way of sneaking past his defenses and getting her way with him.

Birju walked into the room. He walked to Dr. Shastri, and whispered in his ear. "Dinner is served!" exclaimed the septuagenarian.

Saima stood in her room. She felt the warmth of the whisky coursing through her skin. The reddish-brown drink seemed to have unlocked a different plane in her being: a plane where she felt uninhibited to express her deepest desires. Saima stared at the bed in front of her. She knew she would drift off to sleep the instant she hit the bed. There was, however, an impulse that restrained her and forced her to stand upright. She felt an irresistible urge to take a warm shower; it was an urge which needed to be satiated. Saima peeled off the lavender-coloured top of the tracksuit from her broad shoulders and placed it on the bed; she gently pulled her track pants down to the floor. Her bare figure stood silhouetted against the windows of the room, her tender flesh broke into goose bumps sensing the chill in the room.

Saima stepped into the shower. The red light of the geyser unit shone bright, a red bathrobe hung on a hook on the door. Her fingers gently tugged on the shower knob. Droplets of water soon morphed into a steady stream flowing from the showerhead. The flow of water ran across her body, covering each and every inch of her skin. Saima stood below the shower with both her arms embraced across her chest. She could feel a sensation between her legs, a sensation laced with intent of desire. Arousal was not an alien emotion to her, but its intensity tonight was far stronger than what she had ever experienced. She closed her eyes, Narayan's image flashed across her blank mind. Saima placed her right palm between her legs as if trying to calm her sense and bring it back to a neutral state. Slender streams of water flowed seamlessly over her right hand, masking the wetness between her legs.

Narayan lay in his bed wide awake. His mind was analysing the multitude of information that he had processed while viewing the Mughal paintings on his grandfather's laptop. The painting of the lady in black, Jahanara, sitting besides the tomb of Shah Jahan occurred frequently in his mind. There was something about that painting, something the professor's conscious mind could not articulate logically, yet it was an impulse which grew stronger by the minute. He knew he had to act on it; he had to see that image one more time. Narayan got up from his bed, picked up his spectacles and walked out of the bedroom. He took gentle steps trying his best not to disturb the night's calm silence. As he passed Saima's room, he paused for a minute. *Maybe I should inform Saima...tell her about that painting*, deliberated the professor. Narayan bunched his fingers and knocked on her door. "Saima...this is Narayan...do you have minute?" Narayan spoke in a low whisper. A couple of seconds passed without a response. The professor surmised that she was probably asleep and took a step away from the door.

"Hold on...," Saima replied, inside her room.

Narayan stopped and turned back to the door, "I hope I didn't disturb you...were you asleep?"

"No...not really."

The professor could hear the rustle of her anklets, which grew from a faint echo to a resonant sound. Saima opened the door. Her hair, slightly wet from the shower, flowed freely over her shoulders. Beads of water perched on her neck, like early morning dewdrop on leaves of grass. A red bathrobe, tied gently around the waist, wrapped around the contours of her body. Narayan's world faded around him as he took in the sight of Saima Azmi dressed in a bathrobe with a neckline that revealed enough to titillate the senses.

Saima looked deep into Narayan's eyes. The second hand of a table clock in Saima's room ticked away.

16

The bearded man stood smoking near a meat shop.

A broad, thick blade of knife came down in a swift motion; it caught the glint of the late morning sun and cut through the tender meat, halving it in two. The meat bazaar was sparsely crowded with people, but flies, crows, and stray dogs made up the numbers. Vendors seated on plastic stools checked the quality of their meat, running their hands through the firm, but dead, piece of flesh. Thighs, legs, and other succulent pieces of meat hung from hooks stripped of their skin in an attempt to attract buyers. Dried blood was the singular motif of the bazaar as it was found everywhere: from inanimate objects to the clothes worn by meat vendors to their skin. The man turned his gaze across the market. He saw a plump old woman chasing away a couple of crows trying to fly away with a discarded piece of liver hanging from its claws. In another corner, a stray dog feasted on shiny white piece of bone, which it held between its paws while its mouth contorted to get the best out of the bone. Smelling a treat, another stray dog ventured near the bone. The meat bazaar soon filled with barks and howls of the two dogs as they fought for the bone.

The bearded man thought of the meat bazaar in his hometown. Compared to the one in front of his eyes, the bazaar back home was a sterile, sophisticated place. There would be no traces of blood found anywhere; no flies 'crows' strays; vendors sliced pieces of meat in a gentle manner and handed it over to customers packaged in butter paper. The whole process seemed to resemble an orchestra performing a well-practised symphony. It would have been difficult to tell the difference between a bakery and the bazaar.

His father would visit the bazaar on Sundays and bring back fresh meat, which would then be stewed and served with loaves of wheat bread.

The bearded man took a puff from his cigarette and watched the butcher chop a meaty thigh into medium-sized pieces. It reminded him of his father being shot multiple times in a street market by men wearing green camouflage.

A stray piece of the meat jumped from the blade, red with blood, and landed on the face of the bearded man. The butcher smiled, his teeth stained with red paan, and offered an apology. The man flicked the stray piece off his face, and stubbed his cigarette, blowing out the smoke. He looked up and saw Captain Veer dressed in a black suit standing a few feet away staring at him. The officer took a few steps and walked towards him. The bearded man turned inside the bazaar and walked with a fast cadence through its long corridor. He picked up a knife placed on a chopping board and continued to walk. In one corner of the bazaar, a butcher took a chicken out from its coop. The bird fluttered and struggled to escape the grasp of its captor. Holding it down firmly on his chopping block, the butcher severed the neck of the chicken in one swift motion of his blade. The bearded man looked back to see if the officer was following him or not. He saw Captain Veer trying to catch up with him. His footsteps increased their pace. The bearded man bumped against another customer, shoved him aside, and continued to walk. The customer mouthed expletives in the direction of the man walking away. He soon reached the end of the bazaar. Stepping out on the road, he glanced back one more time, the officer was nowhere in sight. He took a deep breath and turned back. For a moment, he did not believe what he saw: Major Rathore stood a few feet away from the man, dressed in a black suit. Instincts kicked in, and the bearded man began running to his left, at full tilt, with the knife in hand. He raced past a shop selling old radios, a cycle repair shop, and a ladies tailor. The street, a back alley to an arterial road, was deserted at the time of the day. Huffing and puffing, the bearded man stopped at a turning in the street. With his hands on his knees, he gasped for breath. A couple of minutes passed. When his breath steadied, he looked up. Veer Pratap Singh stood a few feet away from him. The man collected himself and raised his knife. The Captain raised his 9mm revolver. The bearded man lowered his knife and threw it down.

A near empty room with walls painted off-white, no windows and no ventilation. Sockets of bright white light, placed at equal intervals on the ceiling, lit up the room. The bright light washed out any shadows that may have inhabited the room. A deep silence filled the room, amplifying the slightest of sounds. The bearded man ran his clean, soft hands through his beard. He sat on a steel chair, not big enough to support his frame, with his right leg over his left knee, his body in a profile to the table and the other two chairs in the empty room. There was a sense of immaculate order about the man. His fingernails were cut and softened around its edges; the nails were clean and white with a hint of pink at its base. The thick beard was trimmed uniformly within a few inches of his square jaw line. Though he wore a faded Pathani suit, it looked neat and tidy despite its age. The only anomaly was his footwear. The white running shoes, which covered his feet, were of a familiar brand and had turned brown and black with passing time. Its sole gently peeled off near the toe; long, thin cracks ran across the heel of the shoe indicative of use and abuse. Dried drops of blood, camouflaged cleverly by the wear and tear of the shoe, lay sprinkled across its face. His deep brown Pathani suit ruffled, as he shifted slightly on the chair. The ruffle echoed through the room. His gaze was firmly fixed on the bottom corner of the wall facing him. Major Rathore and Captain Veer entered the room with a swift push of the black door. Sounds from outside – people walking about, people typing on keyboards, fax machines sprouting out paper copies – trickled inside the silent room and vanished almost immediately as the black door closed shut. The room was like a vacuum amidst a sea of sound. The two officers entered and walked in quick, long strides to their respective chairs. The two chairs for the two officers were broad, cushioned, and shaped ergonomically to support the back. It was designed to provide maximum comfort during long hours of work. Major Rathore took his seat, opened the top button of his black suit, took out a fresh white cigarette packet from the inside pocket of the suit, peeled it open and offered a smoke to the bearded man. Acting on impulse, the man reached out and picked out a stick of cigarette. Before the Major could offer a light, the man produced a lighter and lit his cigarette. The tobacco at the tip burned bright red as the man puffed on it. Thick, white smoke rushed out of his nostrils, but did not dissipate, as was its nature. The smoke collected, resembling a cloud, and hung around. The bearded man's stiff posture relaxed immediately.

Black, shiny shoes of the two officers rested on the ground; white, rundown running shoes of the bearded man rested awkwardly on the ground.

"Why were you following us?" Captain Veer spoke, breaking the silent equilibrium of the room, as he sat on his chair.

The bearded man took a long puff and released it slowly, adding to the cloud of smoke. "I am training to be a DIA officer, just like you two gentlemen. That's why I have been following you."

Captain Veer unbuttoned the top button of his suit and leaned his elbow on the table. The reflective glass of his wristwatch caught the reflection of the bearded man. He pointed his index finger at him, "You can be a smartass on the streets outside. Here, inside this room," the officer pointed at the table, "*You will* answer our questions," Captain Veer's eyes glowered with a firm tone.

The bearded man glanced at Captain Veer, "If that is what you want, that is what I will do."

"Why were you following us?" Captain Veer repeated his earlier question.

"My name is Badshah Khan. I was tracking your movements."

"Why?" Captain Veer questioned.

"Because we are planning to blow up a few places in New Delhi. Nothing apocalyptic. Just a couple of RDX and pipe bombs in crowded streets for maximum impact," Badshah Khan stated matter-of-factly.

The two officers were taken aback for a moment with this direct and almost instant confession.

Captain Veer took a good look at Badshah Khan who was preoccupied with his cigarette. "If what you are telling is the truth, and you can give us the details of your plan, the law will be lenient with your sentence. Who knows, you may even receive a pardon."

"I am not looking for leniency or pardon," retorted Badshah Khan. "We want vengeance."

"I am confused," Major Rathore spoke for the first time since he entered the room, "If it is vengeance, revenge, that you are looking for, why tell us your plans in the first place?"

Badshah Khan smiled, "Because we want to challenge you. We want to tell you that there is nothing you can do about it. Even if I tell you when and where the explosives will go off, there is nothing the two of you, or anyone in this country, will be able to do about it."

Captain Veer clenched his fists and was about to get up from his chair when Major Rathore placed his hand on the officer's shoulder.

"Since you are of the firm belief that there is nothing we can do about it, why don't you tell us the time and venue of your terrorist acts?"

Badshah Khan took a puff of his cigarette which was fast running out. He tipped the ash off his cigarette in the same manner which had alerted Major Rathore when he saw him at the tea vendor in the feast bazaar. "Imagine a crowded restaurant. People are getting together after work, they laugh, they talk. Waiters rush around tables, taking orders, serving food. There are large groups of office goers, small groups of friends, couples sharing a drink. The place is nearly full. Two women walk into the restaurant. One of them carries an off-white leather handbag which has dark brown patterns on it. It looks nothing out of the ordinary. The two women take their seats in a corner of the restaurant. A couple of tables put together so that the eatery does not miss out on two customers. They are completely shadowed by a large boisterous group of men and women. One of the women keeps the handbag at the foot of her seat. A waiter comes over soon enough and takes their order: wine and food," Badshah Khan took a puff, the cigarette burnt to its filter tip, "Now imagine a pub which is across the restaurant. Loud music plays in the pub. The volume of the music is matched by the sound of people's conversations. The people are bunched closer together here than in the restaurant. The pub has an equal number of men and women. Some of them move their bodies to the music playing on the speakers, while sipping on their drinks and chewing on tit-bits. The bartender asks a patron whether he will refresh his drink, to which he refuses politely. None of them notice a couple of women entering the pub and taking a seat at the bar. One of the women carries a handbag similar to the one carried by the woman in the restaurant. The woman in the pub places the handbag at the foot of her seat, which is a bar stool. Back at the restaurant, life goes on as usual. People eat, drink, waiters serve. Nothing seems out of the ordinary. The two women keep looking at their handbags as if their lives depended on it. A man sips on his cold beer. A loud explosion is heard opposite the street. Smoke pours out of the pub. The patrons in the restaurant rush out. Fire engines are heard nearing the site. People stop and watch the scene. A waiter from the restaurant assures a customer saying that it was probably a gas cylinder explosion from the kitchen of the pub. Nothing to worry about. The patrons of the restaurant return to their seats. The man returns to his seat and takes another sip of his cold beer when a blast brings down the roof of the restaurant crushing people beneath it," Badshah Kahn dropped his cigarette butt to the floor. "The end."

The room returned to its equilibrium of silence. Badshah Khan sat on his chair, the two officers on theirs. No words exchanged.

Captain Veer quickly glanced at his watch, the second hand ticking away in its relentless march, "Are you telling us that you plan to bomb a restaurant and a pub located opposite to each other?"

"Maybe..."

"No Veer. What this man has told us is a scene that I remember too well, a scene that resembles the bombing sequence from a French black and white movie, *Battle of Algiers*," Major Rathore turned towards his partner, "It is a film that, unfortunately, many separatist groups screen for recruits. The film is screened for its depiction of guerrilla warfare. I think he is leading us on a wild goose chase."

"You are right, Major Rathore," Badshah Khan nodded his head. "But...if you think about it, how is the scene which I just narrated any different from the bombings that have happened in your country or in other parts of the world?"

The two officers looked hard at their suspect.

"Sure...the scene is from a movie, but it doesn't necessarily mean that it cannot happen in real life, or it is not what we plan to carry out soon in your city."

"If you are trying to play with us, there is something you need to understand...we will peel each and every inch of your skin, and rearrange your bone structure in such a manner that no one will be able to recognize you. Not even your father or mother," Captain Veer had an edge to his voice.

Badshah Khan reached out for a fresh cigarette stick and lit it up, blowing smoke upwards. The cloud of smoke had become dense and stretched from one end of the room to another, indicative of the small size of the room. "I watched my father being shot down by men in uniforms, men who were supposed to protect us, protect the innocent. Instead, those men sprayed bullets like kids shooting water from water guns during Holi. Compared to the horror of seeing your father shot down like a rabid dog, everything else feels like situation comedy."

Captain Veer was getting edgy and shifted his weight around in his seat.

"Your threats mean nothing. You can peel me, pierce me, hang me...I knew I was a dead man walking the moment I entered this room. I have come fully prepared," Badhshah Khan dug into the long pockets of his Patahni suit searching for something.

The two officers moved their hands to their gun holsters fearing the worst.

The bearded man removed a palm sized plastic bag tightly wound with bright orange rubber bands, and placed it on the table. Major Rathore and Captain Veer looked at the bag: it contained pirated DVDs of popular American sitcoms.

"Yours gentlemen, for free, if you let me walk out of here," Badshah Khan grinned.

Captain Veer slapped the bag off the table and stood up towering over the bearded man, breathing down on him. The bag flew to a corner in the room, crashing against the wall, and produced a sharp echo which sounded like a gunshot.

"Veer...calm down. Do not let him get to you."

Captain Veer collected himself and sat down in his chair.

Major Rathore trained his gaze on Badshah Khan, "If you think you are the victim here, because men in uniform shot down your father, you are sadly mistaken. Taking innocent lives as vengeance for innocent lives is not justice; it is still murder. And you will be considered a murderer."

"Gentlemen…I am not a murderer…merely a soldier trying to win a war for a cause he truly believes in," Badshah Khan blew out smoke in the direction of the two officers. "In a way, I am not much different from you officers. You fight your war…"

"Make no mistake," Captain Veer cut short Badsah Khan, "We are not like you or like any of your terrorist brethren. We have lost our loved ones too, but we are not carrying bombs in women's handbags, or knapsacks, or backpacks, and exploding it among unsuspecting innocents like cowards. You are not a soldier, you are a coward," the adrenaline rush of anger gripped the officer.

Badshah Khan puffed, then retorted, "And shooting down innocents, raping them, destroying their homes, are acts of valour and courage? Just because you commit your crimes out in the open, in broad daylight, and have the support of your state, doesn't make it any less of a cowardly act."

A tense silence hung around the table, like a ticking bomb.

"I clearly remember the Delhi blasts last year. Our explosives took out everything and everybody…"

"You better stop," Captain Veer's voice was building into an uncontrollable rage.

"I heard that the bodies were burnt and charred beyond recognition. Could you identify the body of your wife, Major Rathore…?"

The ticking bomb exploded.

The Major flew from his chair, over the table, at Badshah Khan. The two landed on the floor with the officer landing punch after punch on the terrorist's square face. The bearded man simply lay smiling. Blood began to ooze from his flesh on to the hairs of his beard, which formed into a drop before dripping down on the floor. Veer was numb, seated in his chair; he had never seen his partner fly into a fit of rage. Major Rathore continued to assault the terrorist, his punches turned into soft thudding echoes floating across the room. Blood had spattered on his white shirt. Captain Veer could not do anything but look on.

It was just another day at one of the Seven Wonders of the World – the Taj Mahal. The early evening sun hung like a golden yellow orb, low in the sky, with a veneer of haze dulling its brightness. Tourists, dressed warmly, streamed through the gardens, walking about leisurely, taking in the sights of the marbled magnificence. Sweepers, men and women, went about their job of raking the blanket of dead yellow leaves which covered the green grass. Trees stood tall, baring their branches, covered with trinkets of leaves which dangled tenderly from its branches. A family of four sat on the soft grass with their legs outstretched and shared a bottle of water. A group of tourists walked about with large hats and dark sunglasses and took pictures from their professional-looking digital cameras. A group of six men laughed and joked loudly as they made their way to the steps of the monument. Another group of four men stood quietly, taking in the sights and sounds. Some of the visitors indulged in taking trick photographs, in perspective, of them holding the tip of the Taj Mahal – a favourite pastime of tourists. A couple of security guards blew their whistles demanding order from the tourists. The early evening scene resembled one of the many landscape paintings of the monument of love.

A couple, fresh from their marriage, and still a little awkward with each other, walked close to the water fountains. The woman wore a deep red sari, her forehead and eyes covered with the sari's brocade. Both her hands were wrapped with red and white bangles, from her wrist till half her forearm. The man was dressed in simple trousers and shirt ensemble. As the couple walked, the man extended his hand in an attempt to take his wife's hand, the woman shrugged slightly; the new husband withdrew his hand midway. Salim Khan observed this delicate dance of marriage courtship. He had heard that it was a tradition for the newly married to visit the Taj Mahal as a good omen which would rub off on their marriage as well and produce an undying love between husband and wife, just like Shah Jahan and Mumtaz Mahal. Khan treated what he heard with a certain amount of cynicism.

Major Khan's cynicism dissipated as soon as he set foot inside theTaj Mahal. He felt an emotion, which he had never experienced before, wash over his senses. His ego, his conscious mind seemed to ebb away leaving him with a profound silence. The silent splendour of the monument entranced him. His eyes took in the intricate Jali work: carvings on marble screens surrounding the tombs of Shah Jahan and Mumtaz Mahal. The subtle artwork on the marble, the beautifully inscribed calligraphy panels, each and every detail came alive and took on a larger significance than being mere artwork. Salim Khan simply stood, with a sense of bliss that enveloped him.

The sense of bliss soon broke when a group sauntered inside. It was headed by a guide who was being his usual eloquent self, educating the tourists on the nitty-gritty's of Shah Jahan's monument of love. Right from the emperor chopping off the fingers of labourers who built the monument to the bodies of Shah Jahan and Mumtaz Mahal facing the direction of Mecca, the guide covered his practised speech with a thick English accent. One member of the group got down on his knees and proposed to his girlfriend. The woman stared hard at her boyfriend with a sense of disbelief before erupting into a loud wail of unbridled joy; kissing and hugging her would be husband. This elicited a loud applause and whistles from other members of the group. A portly security guard came rushing in brandishing his wooden stick with his whistle dangling to and fro. He wanted to know what was happening. The guide calmed the over-exuberant security man and sent him on his way, pushing a fifty-rupee note into his pocket. Salim Khan had a blank expression on his face. He felt a little irritated on the inside that his aura of bliss had been punctured, bringing him down to the inescapable sensation of reality. Khan quietly exited the interior room.

The comfortable shadow of the interiors faded into outdoor light as Major Khan moved into the spacious courtyard that lay between the mausoleum and the mosque: the riverfront terrace. As he walked to the edge of the terrace, flanked by the Yamuna, he observed an old Japanese couple seated on an elevated rectangular platform which contained a water tank in its centre. The couple were dressed in comfortable jeans and cotton jackets. Their legs had protective, bag-like white coverings that most foreigners wore while walking inside the Taj and its surroundings. Shoes and slippers were not allowed inside the monument. The

Major overheard the old man telling his wife that the cenotaphs of Shah Jahan contained an inkwell while that of Mumtaz Mahal contained an empty slate. This was because a woman's heart is considered to be slate where a man writes his desires. The old woman smiled and planted a soft peck on her husband's cheek. The old man blushed slightly and began rubbing the back of his neck. Salim Khan understood what the man was saying as he was fluent in Japanese, one of the many languages that he had learnt in his time at the ISI.

He walked to the edge of the riverfront terrace. The majestic Yamuna came into view leading the Major's eyeline to the horizon. Though he was in the midst of the Taj Mahal – a monument symbolizing eternal love – he had personally never experienced the emotion of romantic love. Salim Khan was the kind of man who had no time to think of anything else except his march to gain absolute power. The only person he cared for with a sense of pure affection was his sister. The thought of his sister made Major Khan close his eyes for a brief moment and thank the Almighty for keeping her alive. When he opened his eyes, he saw the same awkward newly married couple standing a few feet away from him. They seemed to be a little more comfortable around each other now, the man's hand brushed lightly against his wife's bangles. *It is probably the Taj effect*, surmised Major Khan. He had never been a man who attracted the attention of the opposite sex, and even if he did, he was unaware about it. Major Khan turned to face the marble mausoleum and the architectural splendour that lay in front of his eyes: the white Taj Mahal, flanked by the red mosque, with green gardens halved neatly by water fountains lying dead centre, and the red and white coloured Darwaza-i-Rauza (The Great Gate).

Major Khan made his way to the rectangular water tank. The old Japanese couple had moved on to the mosque. He sat on the elevated platform, facing the gardens: Tourists, who made their way to the mausoleum, looked like dots joining to form a line. As he observed the tourists, he wondered what kind of a Mughal Emperor he would make. Would he be like Akbar: fair, just, a uniting force who believed in the greater good, yet a fierce warrior and a brilliant strategist. Would he be like Shah Jahan: build monuments, architectural wonders, encourage the arts, and forward the horizons of the empire. Or would he be like Aurangzeb: canny, cunning like a fox, constantly engaged in conflict to expand the kingdom, but never forgetting the welfare of his subjects, and the best part – devotion to his sister. Major Khan mulled over the thought, and chose Babur. The first Mughal Emperor came closest to a Mughal ruler that Major Khan would make: fearlessly establish a dynasty in a foreign land. Though it did not show on his face, Major Khan experienced an adrenaline rush as he thought about the influence and authority an emperor would yield.

Major Khan was climbing to the top of the ISI. With the west heavily investing in his state for strategic and security purposes, he saw himself as an orchestrator who conducted the fragile, and often hostile politics of the area. It was, however, the same routine day after day: the west would want to carry out an attack on an alleged terror training site or a warehouse which housed militants; the powers that be in the ISI would chalk out a strategy which would not compromise their interests while allowing the west to carry out their attacks. Salim Khan had been successful in alerting the targets of the strikes, causing minimum damage to ISI interests, which required the various militant organizations to carry out its systematic proxy war with its dearly derided neighbour. The minor damages caused during the strikes allowed the west to believe that it had conducted its mission with reasonable success. Major Khan did not find the kind of supremacy he was looking for. He was bored.

Major Khan was an important cog in the fragile geo-politics of the subcontinent; he was consulted by powerful military and political figures from both establishments; yet, he was not the one pulling the strings. He too had to answer and obey a higher authority; an authority which was weak and spineless, which took decisions not because it wanted to, but because it had to. The only thing that would give him total control was anonymity: being able to pull the levers that churn this world while remaining in the shadows. He believed that the men who ran this world were the ones who operated from behind the curtains, rarely stepping into the spotlight. Anonymity allowed the men a greater sense of freedom, than any premier of a nation or the richest man in the world, to control the most potent weapon known to humankind – money. The men who controlled the flow of money in an out of financial institutions, from one stock market to another, from one crisis-ridden country to another, were the men who controlled the course of the world. All others were puppets whose strings these masters pulled. The power resting in the hands of these few men was so complete that its reverberations were felt by each and every living being inhabiting this planet.

This was what led the Major to hunt for the rare diamond. Noor-e-Jahan would be the first step in Major Khan's quest for supreme control. Once he sold the diamond to the highest bidder, he would buy his anonymity. Then, he would be master, he would be emperor.

A stiff cold breeze blew across the Major awakening him from his train of thought. The sun hung low above the horizon. He looked around, the stream of tourists were making their way towards the exit, the Great Gate. Major Khan got up, straightened his pants, buttoned his winter jacket and made his way in the direction of the tourists.

Straight, sharp, brown-coloured toothed-bar of a rake brushed autumn leaves, shed from a tree, towards a secluded spot. Long, narrow fingers guided the rake; the hands of the person sweeping the leaves pierced and pushed it close to the brown bark of a tree where a heap of dried leaves lay. A woollen cap covered the head of the sweeper, which jutted to cover the top of his ears. The man wore a dark green uniform, the shirt of which was worn over a black full-sleeve sweater. His eyes furtively glanced around in a hurried restless manner. He stepped close to the heap, his right hand slid down his zipper and into his crotch. A ubiquitous conical plastic container emerged in his right hand. The sweeper zipped his pants quickly and covered the container with the palm of his left hand. Once again, he glanced around; the tourists streaming out did not pay any attention to the tall lanky man standing next to the bark of the tree. In one quick motion, he dropped the container on the heap of leaves and brushed it over with more leaves. He placed the rake against the tree. It would be at least a couple of days before the heap would be cleared, providing the perfect hiding spot.

A group of tourists slowly made their way out of the interior of the Taj Mahal mosque. The guide seized his opportunity and placed a transparent plastic cube at a secluded corner, in a blind spot of the CCTV cameras. He made his way out of the mosque and ran into a security guard. The guide, with dyed black hair and brown scarf wrapped around his neck, froze for a second. The guard smiled his 100-watt smile, "No more tourists?"

The guide relaxed and replied, "No. I am done for the day. Going home to my wife and my kids."

The guard leaned closer, "Listen...I have a favour to ask of you...my brother-in-law...a bright kid...but he is without a job...Can you recommend him for the job of a local guide," he spoke in a low tone.

"Sure, I will do that..."

The guard shook the guide's hand, "Thank you."

The guide smiled and walked on.

"See you tomorrow."

The guide turned back and replied while walking, "Who knows whether there will be a tomorrow."

Major Khan walked past the security check post and on to the free road. He opened the door of his black sedan, which was stationed at the parking lot, and got into the rear passenger seat. The driver started the engine; the Major removed his wig and peeled off his fake beard: He had been in disguise all the while.

17

The faint reflections of Captain Veer and Major Rathore were sketched on the glass facade of a coffee shop. Logos of the coffee shop – steam rising from a cup of coffee – were embossed across the glass facade providing a thinly veiled blanket of privacy from life on the street outside. Inside, the coffee shop had no more than a few people scattered across its softly lit decor. A group of college students occupied one corner, immersed in a project they were working on. A couple sat with their backs facing the room, whispering sweet nothings: The man ran his hand from the woman's left shoulder to her hips, which he squeezed gently in a playful manner. The woman ran her fingers across the man's hair trying to part it sideways. In the centre of the coffee shop sat a man, slightly obese, who fidgeted with his cell phone. A slender black suitcase sat at the foot of the man's chair. The coffee shop provided the perfect ambience for the two officers: silent enough to hold a conversation, while the pleasant ambient sounds, of the music streaming out of hi-fidelity speakers and of the people in the room, served as a pleasant distraction.

Captain Veer and Major Rathore sat next to the glass facade on a table for two. The laminated circular table had a wooden finish, and was accompanied by two mauve-coloured cushioned chairs. Captain Veer sat erect in his chair wearing the same black suit he had worn earlier during the interrogation. Major Rathore sat with his hands and elbows on the table. The officer had changed into a fresh pair of white full sleeve shirt and black pants; the shirt did not carry any memory or mark of the interrogation. Major Rathore gazed out of the glass facade. Captain Veer looked down at the table as if trying to remember something. The sounds of the coffee shop filled in for the silence between the two officers. The barista soon approached the table: a tall girl with a thin wiry frame, nose and ears pierced with black studs, wearing pink canvas shoes.

"Two cappuccinos please," Captain Veer held up two fingers.

"Would you like anything else sir...something to eat?" the girl bent slightly forward with a twinkle in her eye. "We have an offer running now...if you order..."

"Two cappuccino's please...thank you," the Captain reiterated.

"Okay," the girl forced a smile and left the table.

"Veer...I am..."

"Sir...no need to go down that path...," Captain Veer flashed his palm. "You don't need to explain."

"I don't know what came over me," Major Rathore had a tired look in his eyes. "I knew he was trying to instigate us...but, for some reason, I just couldn't control myself."

The coffee machine in the background hissed, the sound of two cups filling up echoed across the room.

"He thoroughly deserved what he got. Scum like him should be beaten back to the hole they crawl out of."

The girl arrived with a green tray carrying two white cups, each topped with a layer of foam. She placed the tray gently on the table. "Enjoy your coffee," the girl said with a forced smile and left the table.

Captain Veer held the cup in his right hand, between his thumb and index finger and took a sip. Major Rathore held the cup with both his hands, which trembled a bit; the depressions around the knuckles had a reddish glow to them. The warmth of the cup seemed to provide a sense of comfort.

"Are you okay?" Captain Veer looked at his partner.

Major Rathore sipped his coffee and placed his cup on the table, "Well...after taking a sip of coffee, I feel better," he let his gaze rest outside the coffee shop on the road outside.

During the interrogation, Captain Veer was surprised when his partner punched Badshah Khan black and blue. The captain had known his partner and senior, ever since his cadet school days. Major Rathore never lost his temper. He seemed to have a knack for maintaining his calm and composure in any kind of situation. Major Rathore's calm, composed demeanour was the perfect foil to Captain Veer's hot headedness. That is why they made a great team together.

The sudden burst of rage from Major Rathore prompted Captain Veer to take his partner out and talk about it.

Captain Veer eyed the slightly obese man seated in the centre of the room. He was dressed in a black full-sleeve pullover, which was frayed at the edges, with white pants and white shoes. A gold pendant hung on his neck, dangling outside the pullover. An empty coffee cup sat on his table to his right. The officer sensed an odd nervousness about the man, but could not form a concrete thought about it. He shifted his attention back to his partner. "Sir… I know we haven't really talked about the blasts and…," his voice trailed off unable to complete what he wanted to say. "If there is anything you want to talk about, anything at all…"

Major Rathore shifted his attention back to the table. "Veer, you are a good friend. Life has been a little difficult of late. I miss her, especially when I am home. But life goes on…and I am trying to move with it."

A man picked up six empty cups of coffee from the table surrounded by the group of college students. He balanced the six cups on his tray with his left hand, the tips of his fingers spread wide and even underneath the tray, and carried it away from the table.

"Do you think he was being serious about the bomb threat?" Captain Veer looked hard at the table, "About bombing a restaurant and a pub…?"

"The bomb threat may be a real deal. Otherwise, why would he be following us. About the restaurant and the pub…I think he was putting on a show, probably tying to blow smoke in our eyes."

Captain Veer gently blew away the foam and sipped on the dark brown beverage. He caught the slightly obese man leaving from the corner of his eye. "With the US ex-President arriving tomorrow, I was wondering whether we need to alert restaurants and pubs. Especially if they are located one opposite the other."

"Veer…you are forgetting something," Major Rathore took a sip from his cup, "Tomorrow all restaurants and pubs are shut as a protest against the hike in service tax."

Captain Veer rubbed the back of his neck, "Yeah…you are right. I did forget about it."

"Let us just focus on our security detail for the visit. If a situation should arise, we will deal with it th…"

"Sir…that suitcase might be a bomb…call DIA…" Captain Veer sprinted out of the coffee shop leaving Major Rathore in a flummoxed state.

The Major placed his cup of coffee on the table, got up from his chair and walked a couple of steps towards the sleek black suitcase. As he neared the rectangular case, he could a faint ticking sound. "Everybody out of the shop *now…*"

The baristas, the group of college students, and the couple stared hard at the officer.

"There's a bomb here!…everybody out, now!" Major Rathore roared.

A girl screamed, a coffee cup fell to the ground and broke. In a matter of seconds, the room emptied of its inhabitants.

Major speed dialled 1 on his phone, "This is Major Rathore. I need a bomb disposal unit ASAP..."

Captain Veer had sprinted out of the coffee shop in pursuit of the slightly obese man. The man entered the open parking lot of the coffee shop; his keys, dangling on his thumb, caught the glint of the setting sun. The sole of Captain Veer's shiny black shoes hardly touched the ground as it flew on top of the tarmac. The officer ran at full tilt to his left, to the parking area. Captain Veer entered the area only to find an empty square filled with white rectangular lines, denoting spaces for vehicular parking, which stared back at him. The square parking area, which abutted the coffee shop, had thick walls covering it with an opening to the highway that lay behind the officer. It was impossible for anyone to disappear from a dead end, let alone a man with weight issues. There was no trace of the slightly obese man in black pullover and white pants. Not even a footprint. Like steam rising from a hot cup of coffee, he had dissipated into thin air. Captain Veer turned and sprinted back to the coffee shop. The officer had missed a large manhole cover that lay in the right hand corner of the parking area perfectly camouflaged to the colour of the tarmac, which lay ajar by a hair's breadth.

The red glow of a beacon shone bright against a twilight sky. The black van of the bomb disposal unit made its way to the coffee shop followed by a couple of police vans. A few yards away from the coffee shop, the baristas had huddled together, the group of college students were clicking photos from their mobile phones, and the couple held on to each other as if they had experienced a near-death incident. Major Rathore stood a few feet away from the couple. Memories of last year's bomb blasts were running fresh in his mind like a film. With the timely evacuation, he knew another crisis had been averted. The US ex-President was landing in New Delhi the next day. A terrorist act on the eve of the visit would have embarrassed the Government and put a question mark on the country's ability to secure itself. Captain Veer joined his partner. The Captain was taking deep breaths to normalize his heartbeat.

"There was no trace of him..."

Major Rathore had a puzzled expression. "No trace of whom?"

"No trace of the man who planted the suitcase," Veer Pratap Singh straightened his suit.

"Veer, how did you know the suitcase is a bomb?"

"The man looked at his suitcase just before he left the coffee shop. He had not forgotten the suitcase, it was placed there deliberately."

"That is why you are one of the best at DIA," Major Rathore patted his partner's shoulder. "The bomb disposal unit is on its way..."

"I see it," replied Captain Veer between deep breaths.

The black van came to a stop near the two officers. A moustachioed man with an army crew cut stepped out of the van wearing a bright grey suit. His hands were covered with flexible but large white gloves, his feet sported thick white shoes. A tubular headgear fitted with a black visor rested in his left hand. The headgear was the same colour as the suit.

"Ram Singh, it is a black suitcase kept in the centre of the room. Probably has a timer attached to it," Major Rathore informed the man in the grey suit.

"Sir, I am a little surprised…If a bomb is kept to explode in a public place; the timer is set for a maximum of two to five minutes. It has been close to ten minutes since we got the call," Ram Singh slipped on his headgear, flashed a thumbs up sign to the officers and began to walk towards the coffee shop. His breathing echoed inside the suit. Every step he took made a soft noise when the white shoes walked on the grey tarmac. The man in the suit moved as fast as he could.

As the bomb disposal expert walked to the coffee shop, constables who had arrived in the police van began to divert traffic away from the area.

The door of the coffee shop gently parted open. Ambient music was still playing in the room; however, it did not reach the ears of Ram Singh who could only hear his breathing. His grey suit was a stark oddity amidst the soft lights of the coffee shop. The man trained his sight to the centre of the room and located the suitcase. It rested at the foot of the chair: calm, peaceful. Singh took a couple of steps when a barista walked nonchalantly into his line of sight wiping his wet face with a handkerchief. The barista lowered his handkerchief and froze in his stride looking at the man in the grey suit.

Outside, a barista asked aloud, "Where's Amar?"

Amar, a barista working in coffee shop, had dozed off in the restroom located inside the shop. He was oblivious to the bomb scare in the shop, fast asleep when the other baristas and the customers vacated the shop. Amar had woken up from his siesta a few minutes ago and wanted to hurry back to his station.

Inside the coffee shop, the bomb disposal expert and the barista stood, staring at each other. Seconds ticked away on a circular wall clock. Ram Singh began to gesticulate wildly to the barista to get out of the shop shouting, "Bomb! Bomb! Get out! Get out!" Though the barista could not hear what the man was saying, he realized the gravity of the situation. His body reacted, breaking into a run. Amar slipped, but regained his balance and ran out of the shop.

The bomb disposal expert took a deep breath and began walking towards the briefcase. Seconds ticked away on the circular wall clock. Ram Singh stood at the table. He removed one of his safety gloves and reached into his pocket with his bare hand. Out came a laughing Buddha. Ram Singh placed his lucky charm on the floor; it began to swing back and forth. The safety glove back on, he kneeled down slowly. He caught the handle of the briefcase with his right hand and placed it gently on the floor using his left hand to support it. Singh ran his right hand around the periphery of the briefcase to check for trip wires. He took a yellow square scanner from his suit pocket and placed it above the number pad of the suitcase located below the handle.

The scanner did not indicate the presence of any ignition switch or trip wire under the number pad. Beads of sweat began to form on Ram Singh's neck. He was breathing hard inside the suit. Seconds ticked away on the circular wall clock; the laughing Buddha swayed back and forth. Seven...eight...two was the combination on the number pad. Singh turned the combination back to zero...zero...zero. The levers of the suitcase sprang open; the grey suit took a step back. Seconds ticked away on the circular wall clock; the laughing Buddha swayed back and forth. His hands reached out to the sides of the briefcase and slowly lifted the top, inch by inch, from its groove. Seconds ticked away on the circular wall clock. Ram Singh opened the briefcase and peered inside. What he saw made him smile. The laughing Buddha swayed back and forth.

Outside, crowds had begun to form on the side of the road opposite to the coffee shop. The media van of a news channel was parked in the vicinity with a reporter briefing the newsroom about developments: Phrases such as 'bomb threat' and 'democracy under attack' were repeated in clinical fashion by the reporter.

Major Rathore wondered how quickly a crowd had appeared from nowhere. The coffee shop was located in a sparsely populated area along a highway on the outskirts of the city. The shop had a warehouse and an abandoned manufacturing unit for neighbours. There were no residential buildings within eyesight, and yet a crowd had emerged creating a buzz around the area. Then, there was the news channel. The Major could never understand how news channels got wind of such incidents. He mused whether they knew what was going to happen even before the intelligence agencies did.

Ram Singh emerged from the coffee shop with his protective headgear in the right hand and the black suitcase in his left hand. A wave of excitement passed over the news reporter as she reported about the incident facing her cameraperson. The bomb disposal expert walked slowly towards Major Rathore and Captain Veer.

"Either he has diffused the bomb successfully and is showing off…or he has lost his nuts and is going to blow us up all the way to heaven," remarked Captain Veer.

Ram Singh took a minute to reach the two officers. Night had fallen; the highway and its surroundings were bathed in the yellow of streetlights. Singh arrived and stood facing Major Rathore and Captain Veer. He extended his left hand towards Major Rathore, "Sir, please open the suitcase."

Captain Veer whispered in his partner's ears, "Do not take the suitcase. I am sure he has lost his marbles."

Major Rathore took the suitcase and kneeled down on the tarmac on one knee placing the suitcase on the ground. The Major flipped the levers of the briefcase and lifted the top. A plastic alarm clock sat in the middle of the suitcase, ticking away, surrounded by pirated DVDs of Hindi films. The briefcase was brimming with the DVDs, some of which spilt over to the tarmac.

"Sir, it was either a prank or a hoax," Ram Singh explained.

*Satyamev...satyamev...satyamev jayate...*Captain Veer's phone rang. The officer answered the phone immediately. "Officer..."

"Captain Veer...this was just a hoax," said the low guttural voice over the phone

Captain Veer switched his phone to speaker mode.

"Imagine what would have happened if the briefcase was a live bomb..."

The line went dead.

Smoke began to blow out of the briefcase. Major Rathore quickly got up on his feet from the kneeling down position and backed off along with his partner and Ram Singh. The alarm clock struck 12; the briefcase burst into flames.

Thick yellow flames lit up the faces of the two officers as the briefcase burnt brightly.

18

Major Khan stood by the large glass window of his hotel room and looked down on the street below. His forehead rested lightly on the glass while his body leaned away from the window.

The man and his reflection on the glass window formed an inverted 'v'. Life streamed on the street below without a pause: vehicles moved forward, people walked about, and lights which illuminated the night stood perfectly still. To Major Khan, life unfolding on the streets seemed small and insignificant, as if he was watching a bustling city of ants. For a moment, he wondered if this was how the almighty felt when he watched his creations from the heavens. The Major had a smile playing on his lips. His phone began to buzz in his pant pocket. Without shifting his forehead from the glass window, he removed his phone and looked at its screen. As soon as he saw the number, he straightened his posture and answered the call.

"Ji Janaab…The briefcase worked brilliantly…The officers did not have a clue…It has created a perfect diversion for our fireworks…They may have won many wars, but tomorrow, by the grace of the Almighty, we will be the victors…," Major Khan disconnected his phone; he slouched on a sofa placed next to the window.

Major Khan was dressed in a burgundy turtleneck paired with cream cotton pants topped with a knitted black v-neck sweater. He relaxed his eyes, rubbing them gently with his index fingers. The room was sparsely furnished: a single bed draped with clean, fresh covers, a black woollen blanket folded neatly at the foot of the bed, a circular table, and the sofa in which the Major lounged. Apart from the coffee maker that sat on the table next to the sofa, the only other apparatus in the room was a heater which hummed a pleasant low drawl, providing a relaxing ambient sound to the small room.

Major Khan checked his phone; he was hoping to hear from Safi. He mused over the memory of Safi excitedly telling him about the *Noor*. When he received the letter from his sister, Major Khan wondered whether someone was playing a prank on him. It was only when she called him up and spoke to him reassuring him of her well being, that he felt a sense of normalcy return to his life. Safi had confided in her brother her discovery of the letter in their storage room. She told him about the possible existence of a diamond that surpassed Koh-i-Noor. This was what Major Khan had wanted to hear: a launching pad to his quest for absolute power. Mention of the diamond set Major Khan's mind ticking...If there was even a measure of truth to Safi's story, there would be no stopping him.

Major Khan tilted his head back and went over his plan. Get the diamond, sell it, move abroad, create a new identity, control guerrilla groups and the fragile political climate at home with his newly acquired weapon – money; use money to lure the powers in his homeland to do his bidding, when the west came calling, which was just a matter of time, ask for accounts in Swiss Banks to do their dirty work....

The plan seemed perfect to Major Khan.

He sat up in the sofa, his eyes wandered around the empty, silent room. The emptiness of the room guided his thoughts back to Safi Bano. At times, he mused whether the letter and the phone call were just figments of his imagination: a way for his mind to cope with the grim reality of Safi's death. He had not met her since she went to London for her architecture degree. Major Khan's phone buzzed distracting his train of thought. It was a message from Safi; it read: In Agra, one step close to the *Noor.*

His sister was alive and well.

The stiff white paper sat straight on a desk surrounded by two vertical rows of metal drawers. Madan Shastri's brows furrowed as he scanned the black printed ink on the paper. The retired army man was at the Directorate of Military Intelligence (MI). He was at his desk reading a report on the bombings that had taken place in a cathedral, a popular tourist destination, in a metropolitan European city. The blasts had caused the entire east wing of the cathedral to collapse. Many were dead, many more injured. The incident had taken place barely a few hours ago. Madan Shastri had received a call from Major Rathore who informed him about the bomb hoax. A father's intuition told him that Narayan could face a similar threat on his quest for the Noor-e-Jahan. He feared for the safety of his son and had arrived at MI to tap into any vital information he could lay his hands on.

The wrinkled fingers of Madan Shastri twirled a transparent paperweight embedded with coloured dots on his desk. Images of men and women screaming, black smoke billowing, broken streets, charred dead bodies, flashed across his eyes. The cathedral blasts worried him. Such a blatant attack on a popular tourist destination, which had round the clock security, could be easily duplicated in a vast and diverse country. Madan Shastri looked around him; there was a multitude of information arriving almost every minute. Printers and faxes worked tirelessly churning out intelligence reports; screens of laptops and desktops displayed information regarding impending acts of terror. Most of the information was spam, of no particular consequence; however, there would always be a couple of reports that signalled a real threat. Trying to extricate the reports that predicted an act of terror from the deluge of information was the tricky part, like locating a needle in a haystack. In spite of the insurmountable odds, the intelligence agencies regularly briefed the security apparatus about impending acts of terrorism. The incidents that did take place were due to the lax policing efforts, the lieutenant general believed.

The MI unit filled with sounds of keyboards typed, of drawers opened and closed, footsteps that walked about, landline phones that rang, but no human sound.

A hand gently tapped the retired army man's shoulder and placed another stiff white paper on Madan Shastri's desk. He smiled at the person who brought the paper as a sign of his appreciation. Madan Shastri looked at the new report; he read the printed black ink again and again as if confirming the information on the report. His eyes widened. The report read: *Terror attack imminent on Taj Mahal. IED explosives may be used.*

Madan Shastri wondered if this was a practical joke.

19

A white marble bench holds two lovers: a prince and a courtesan. The prince is dressed in cream-coloured sherwani suit, embedded with shimmering drops of white pearls. The courtesan is draped in a blood-red salwar kameez with silver, tear-shaped motifs.

She rests her head on his lap. A red chunri covers her face partially, resting on the ridge of her nose, just above her red lips. The prince looks into her eyes, his hand placed on the crown of her head. A large tree stands tall over the two lovers, its leaves guarding their privacy from prying eyes.

The marble bench sits amidst a garden in summer bloom: Blue, yellow, and magenta hued flowers dot the bottle green bushes lining the periphery of the garden, injecting colour and fragrance. Manicured grass lie at the feet of the lovers releasing fresh dew drops. Fountains of water run across the centre of the garden, its satin waters ebbing and flowing. The gentle chirpings of birds resonate across the garden landscape.

A blue sky, marked with thin strips of white clouds that turn gold with the rays of the rising sun, is the dome under which the prince and the courtesan have immersed their souls and bodies.

The two lovers lost in one another do not see the large tree behind them transform into a man, soaking in black, carrying a silver tipped sword. The man's deep shadow falls on the white marble bench, on the prince and the courtesan. The silver tipped sword rises high and comes down on them without a sound. It is meant to separate the bond between the lovers, but it strikes an empty marble bench. The man and his woman transform into a pair of doves and fly away to the open sky. The sword breaks into a million little pieces which scatter across the green grass like bright, shining diamonds.

Saima's eyes opened, her heartbeat was racing, and her breathing was shallow and hard. Tiny beads of perspiration sat on the small of her neck. It was the same dream once again.

Saima tried to calm herself down by reminding herself that she was in her bed in a room which was part of Dr. Sharma's row house. She tilted her head sideways; she saw the first rays of a new morning.

Captain Veer sat on the edge of his bed, his head drooping slightly between his broad shoulders. The digital alarm clock on the bedroom table displayed the digits 5 and 30. He looked down at his feet; in the low early morning light, he could make out that his nails were clipped and cleaned. The Captain took a couple of deep breaths to focus his attention and wake his mind from its groggy state. Captain Veer brought his hands to his knees and began rubbing them gently in a circular manner. After a couple of seconds, he got up and slipped his feet into home-wear slippers, the left foot first then the right. Taking slow, easy steps, he trudged to the bathroom. The white tiled bathroom reflected a dull shine as the officer switched on the white light. He grabbed his white toothbrush, squeezed coin-sized portion of fluoride toothpaste on top of the slightly faded bristles, and switched on the geyser. The white head of the toothbrush moved in a circular fashion; Veer counted the number of times the brush moved: ten rotations up, ten rotations down, then, ten rotations up, ten rotations down on the other side. He gargled with water and spat it out into the sink. The water faucet was turned on; a thick stream of warm water began filling a blue bucket. Vapours of steam jumped and danced around the mouth of the water faucet. Veer stepped out of the bathroom, unbuttoned his night suit, folded it and kept it at the foot of the bed before stepping into the bathroom again. The bucket was almost full, Veer turned the water faucet shut. He took a white mug, dipped it into the bucket of water, and poured it over his head and onto his body. The officer repeated this a couple of times until his entire frame was soaking wet with droplets of water. He squeezed blue bathing gel onto his palms and rubbed it over his body, paying conscious attention to it.

Veer stepped out of the bathroom towelling his hair dry. Freshly ironed white shirt and black pants sat on his bed. He dressed quickly, combed his hair, and made his way to the kitchen. His wife was in the kitchen brewing tea. Eggs were kept to boil on the second burner; a toaster ticked away.

"Good Morning,"Veer hugged Swati.

"Good Morning...your breakfast will be ready in five minutes. Have a cup of tea in the meanwhile."

Veer Pratap nodded his head.

Swati poured steaming hot tea through a strainer into a smallish steel cup, which had its mouth open outwards for the fingers to hold it. Veer took his cup and walked out gently to the dining table.

This was Captain Veer's routine on the day he had a special task at hand. The US ex-President was arriving in New Delhi, on his way to the Taj Mahal. Captain Veer and Major Rathore were in charge of managing the security cover throughout the US ex-President's trip. On such days, the officer would go through his morning ritual in a particular order, paying minute attention to it, as a way of staying calm. This way there would be no nerves, no butterflies in the stomach, and Captain Veer could simply focus on the task at hand.

Swati brought the boiled eggs and toasted brown bread to the table. Captain Veer took a bite of the boiled egg, then, took a bite of the toast.

Major Rathore closed the door of his apartment behind him. He had his own way of dealing with a day that required him to be at the top of his game. Unlike his partner, who fussed over the tiniest details of his morning routine, Major Rathore would distract himself by getting out of his house as early as possible and taking as much time as he possibly could to reach the office. On such days, he would walk to DIA Headquarters, located a good 15 kilometres from his house, and take in the sights and sounds of his city waking up.

The Major stood on the pavement and took in the early morning of a winter day. There was a cloud which bathed the city in shades of grey. Bare branches of trees stood out, awaiting summer and life. Men on bicycles criss-crossed the street carrying either newspapers or milk cartons. Major Rathore was dressed in his uniform – black suit with a plain white shirt – which provided a contrast against the grey city.

Major Rathore made his way to a tea stall which was opening up. He had walked close to twenty minutes. The vendor had lit his gas stove and was pouring a packet of fresh milk into his large brass pot. The blue flame springing straight from the black gas burner heated the pot, as the vendor, dressed in a khaki-coloured sweater and monkey cap stirred the liquid content of the pot. The tea vendor and his apparatus provided the lone shade of colour on this particular winter morning.

The vendor handed the officer his first cup of tea in a white plastic cup. Major Rathore took a careful sip of the hot, sweet brew. The first thought that flashed across his mind as he sipped on tea was when he had noticed Badshah Khan following him while having his cup of tea. The officer checked around to make sure no one was following him this time. He took another sip and reminisced about the past few days. The sighting of Major Salim Khan, Object No. 27 going missing and being retrieved by Saima; professor Shastri applying his expertise to solve the link between the missing museum piece and Major Khan, clues unearthed at Sher Mandal, Lodi Gardens and the mobile phone; it all seemed to pass by him like pages of a book. The officer wondered for a second if he was a protagonist of a thriller:

trying to find a lost diamond, hunting down an ex-ISI officer, protecting the premier of a western nation. Two men arrived at the tea stall on a bike. This broke Major Rathore's train of thought. The Major took a final sip and crushed the plastic cup, disposing it in a wicker basket placed near the stall. The plastic cup was the waste basket's very first occupant. Major Rathore paid the vendor and continued his walk to the headquarters. Eyes of the two men who had arrived on the bike followed the officer. One of the men took out a phone and dialled.

Captain Veer waited for his partner at his desk. The DIA was empty this early in the morning; the digital clock on his desk showed 6:58. Major Rathore entered the office. "Good Morning...am I late?"

"Good Morning. We are on time. Let us go," Captain Veer got up from his desk and walked towards the door.

White gauze bandages with dried blood marks lay unwrapped on a tray cover. A middle-aged portly nurse wrapped a fresh bandage gently across a square face. Red dots of blood blotted on the fresh white gauze as it settled on the face. The nurse finished the dressing, picked up the tray cover and walked away. Badshah Khan had been admitted to a military hospital after Major Rathore flew into a fit of rage during the interrogation. The terror suspect had received deep gashing wounds all over his face along with a broken nose. It was decided that Badshah Khan would be hospitalized and kept under 24-hour surveillance. He could prove to be a vital source once he recovered.

A thick white window sat on top of the bed. A single fly, which was staggering around, headed straight into a neon coloured bug zapper and gave the hospital room its final sound. Nothing moved in the room, there was a sense of total silence.

The room was a private cabin with white flooring and white walls. Not a single speck of dust or debris could be found in the room. It was a room devoid of excess. A hospital bed lay in the centre of the rectangular room and a heater occupied a corner of the room. Outside, two police constables stood at attention with sten guns in their hands. Inside, the stationary figure of Badshah Khan moved slightly. He parted his lips and whispered, once again, breaking the deafening silence in the room, "T..aj Mah..al...Taj Mahal..."

"Do you believe in dreams?"

Narayan gazed at the road ahead from behind his car's windshield. Saima waited for a response.

"Narayan..."

Narayan looked at Saima. She looked at him eagerly awaiting a reply.

"I'm sorry...did you ask something?"

"Do you believe in dreams?"

"Dreams as in...having a dream to succeed in something...or dreams that occur at night?"

"I have been having the same dream for a few days now. A courtesan and her lover, a prince; the setting is a royal garden in the bloom of spring. The two lovers are lost in themselves, and lost to the world around them. A man barges in; he is probably the father of the prince. He removes his sword from its sheath, raises it up in the air and brings it down on the two lovers. The sword hits empty ground..."

"The lovers transform into white doves and fly away," Narayan Shastri adjusted his spectacles.

Saima had a surprised look on her face, "How did you know about my dream?"

"This dream…you had it when you stayed over at my place… Remember, you told me about it the next morning."

Saima smiled and shook her closing her eyes in slight embarrassment, "Yes, I did, didn't I… I forgot about it. Narayan, you seem to have a mnemonic memory."

Narayan smiled, "So, what about the dream you've been having?"

Saima gazed out of the car window, "Do you think this dream that I am having," she paused, "Could it mean something?"

Rows of bare boned winter trees glided over the corners of the windshield, one by one.

"When I was a kid," the professor turned slightly to face Saima, "I had this recurring dream…or nightmare if you could call it that."

Saima shifted her body slightly towards Narayan.

"Every night I would have this dream where I walked along green fields with knee high grass swaying gently in the breeze. Flowers bloomed all over the fields. It felt like paradise. Clear blue skies, soft sunshine, red apples dangling about…As I walked along the fields, happy and tranquil… a green snake would leap out of nowhere and bite my neck. I would wake up with a scream."

Narayan eased back in his driving seat. "This dream recurred every night…for close to a month. And then, I stopped having it."

"How old were you when you had your nightmares?"

"I must be six…or seven…," Narayan made minute movements with his hands on the steering wheels, as if trying to correct it to drive in a perfect straight line. "I am not sure whether the dream I had as a kid meant anything."

Saima was lost in thought; her deep brown eyes stared at a bare tree in the distance.

"Coming back to your dream," the professor looked at Saima, "What part about it is troubling you?"

"Hmm…," Saima sighed, "I can't really put my finger on it… maybe it is the prince's father who wants to separate the two lovers…Thinking about it makes me melancholic. Almost as if it is a warning sign, that I may be separated from the man I love," She looked at Narayan. "Since this dream has been playing in my sleep for a few days now, I wonder if it will come true."

The professor placed his left hand on Saima's right hand, "The way I see it, the prince and his courtesan escape, to be united forever, perhaps in a different life or a different form."

"Hmm…That is one way of looking at it," Saima gazed at his hand now back to hold the steering wheel.

Narayan and Saima were on their way back to New Delhi. Their search for a clue amongst Dr. Sharma's exhaustive collection of Mughal art and architecture had drawn a blank. The professor and Saima decide to go back. When the professor took leave of his grandfather earlier in the morning, the septuagenarian had whispered in his grandson's ear to marry Saima, they would make a great couple together. The professor could only smile. Over the past few days, he had begun to feel in a certain way about Saima. He, however, felt it was too early to give a name to that feeling. As the two drove out of the Dr. Sharma's gate, the grandfather wished Saima goodbye, and hoped to see her again soon with Narayan, which was followed by a wink.

Saima smiled as she remembered the goodbye from Dr. Sharma.

"Your grandfather is a great person to be with. I can't imagine anyone having a dull moment around him."

"Yeah…even at this age, he is a bundle of energy and joy. But that's the way I have always remembered him. Since I was a kid."

"Dr. Sharma's collection of Mughal images amazed me. I have never seen such an exhaustive compilation. I could just look over the images again and again for days on end."

"I think his compilation has opened a door for us. Just that I'm not able to figure out which door yet."

"Hmm…There is one image that has lingered on in my memory and stayed with me. The woman, dressed in black, kneeling at the tomb; though her face was partially covered, it still conveyed a sincere emotion of loss."

"You may not believe this, but the painting you are talking about, Jahanara Begum at Shah Jahan's tomb, is an image that I have been thinking about ever since I saw it."

A look of excitement crossed Saima's face. "Narayan, do you think…"

Professor Shastri adjusted the frame of his spectacles, "My gut feeling is that painting is our next clue. Only if I could crack its code…"

The wide eyelids of Saima closed; she tried to recollect the painting from her memory. Few seconds later, she opened her eyes and reached for her backpack kept on the rear passenger seat. Saima zipped open the bag and removed her scribbling pad. When Narayan had shown the image to her for the first time, she had observed the Persian script embedded on the mural, below the woman and the tomb. Saima flipped open the pages of her pad to the page where she had written down the script. Her lips moved silently reading the script over and over again. "Narayan…

the bond that existed between Shah Jahan and Jahanara Begum was deep, right?"

"Absolutely. Jahanara was Shah Jahan's favourite," replied Shastri. "She was his first born and after Mumtaz Mahal passed away, the emperor showered everything on his daughter."

Saima smiled. "Professor Shastri...I think I may have cracked the code. The Noor-e-Jahan went from Shah Jahan to Jahanara."

Captain Veer glanced around pensively. The wide, open arrival hall at the international airport came into view. It was sparsely populated for a weekday morning. Most international flights took off at night, that's when the terminals would be abuzz with people, children, and flight announcements. The Captian preferred it this way: silent and empty. They would be able to whisk away the US ex-President and his wife to their vehicle with the minimum of fuss.

Brightly clothed janitors, security personnel and about a handful of passengers dotted the indoor landscape. A vendor at a magazine stall yawned his heart out, then got back to staring at the ceiling. *So far...so good...*Captain Veer comforted himself. Major Rathore was by his side staring out at the runway. The US ex-President's chartered flight stood like a lone white bird on the tarmac runway. The white door popped open, heads of the US ex-President and his wife bobbed out. They were followed by four security guards – personal bodyguards of the visitor. The elderly couple made the short walk from the runway to the sliding gate of the arrival hall. Captain Veer glanced around, once again, to make sure there was nothing out of place.

The two DIA officers greeted the dignitaries and quickly guided them out of the arrival hall.

A passenger wearing a bandana cap and dressed in black sweater and green jeans followed the sight of the officers and the dignitaries walking away. The passenger was lounging in the waiting hall. He took out his cell phone and dialled.

The US ex-President and his wife had come to India as the couple wanted to celebrate forty years of wedded bliss by visiting the Taj Mahal. What better way to celebrate the love for one another than at the most famous symbol of love. Earlier in the morning, the couple had flown in from China, landed at Delhi airport, and was now on their way to Agra, and to Taj Mahal.

Major Rathore was at the wheel of a dust-brown SUV, driving down the Yamuna Expressway. The US ex-President was travelling in his security vehicle, which was a few meters ahead of the DIA officials. He had requested minimum security cover for his trip to the Taj. Captain Veer thought it was probably the best way to go about it. The US ex-President used to be the most powerful man in the world during his term at the White House in the late eighties. Now, he did not occupy the front pages as he once used to. Since public memory is short, Captain Veer felt that the dignitary and his wife could slip in and out of the Taj Mahal without attracting a lot of attention. There was no special security measures made at the marbled monument as well. Like everyone else, the visitors would take in the sights of the Mughal wonder; the only difference being the presence of four bodyguards who looked like professional body builders. Captain Veer looked at the road ahead; he could see the security vehicle carrying the dignitaries up ahead in the distance. The officer kept his sight firmly on the road ahead.

Narayan drove his sedan to a stop outside the grand Delhi Gate at Agra fort. The giant, red sandstone gate stood tall above the navy blues sedan, dwarfing it. Narayan and Saima stepped out of the car; a group of ASI officials were waiting at the entrance of the gate.

Narayan and Saima were halfway to Delhi when Saima told professor about the Persian script in the mural. The mural was engraved inside the Musamman Burj at Agra Fort. The two decided to see the mural and confirm Saima's breakthrough regarding the Noor-e-Jahan. Narayan called his grandfather and revealed to him the latest development. Dr. Sharma urged his grandson to proceed to Agra Fort immediately.

"Hi. I am Narayan Shastri. This is Saima Azmi. Thanks for having us over on such short notice," Professor greeted the officials.

"Anything for Dr. Sharma," replied a portly figure who seemed to be the head of the group. He greeted Narayan and Saima. Narayan noticed that his lower-lip was stained dark red. The stain indicated that the man had a habit of eating tobacco-filled paan. His shoes had cracks, which ran from the soles to the flat head of the shoe, displaying signs of the weight it bore from day-to-day. The man's wrinkled forehead was neatly divided by a vermilion line. He was meeting the professor for the first time; however, he had seen Saima once before; at the museum, when she, in a fit of inspiration had not noticed the same portly figure walk away with Object No. 27.

Narayan and Saima were guided inside Delhi Gate and entered Agra Fort. The two walked at a fast cadence, Saima's anklets rustling along, followed by the group of ASI officials. The group made their way to Musamman Burj: a tower carved out of pure white marble, perched right on top of the red Agra Fort, which gave a clear and unobstructed view of the shimmering Taj Mahal sitting pretty on the horizon.

The professor soon found himself inside the very heart of the beautifully carved marble tower. Red, green, and blue coloured precious stones speckled the white marble walls; intricate pietra dura accompanied the precious stones as the decorative art ran across walls and pillars. All this splendour was lost on Narayan as he focused his complete attention on finding the Jahanara mural. It was only when he stepped onto the balcony of the tower did he find his attention melt away to accommodate the sight of the Taj. Yes, the professor had seen the symbol of eternal love, from the inside and the outside. Yet, the view he had from Musamman Burj did not compare with any of his previous experiences. The symbol of love seemed like a full, shining moon on a clear night.

"Prof....Prof...," Saima's voice broke the professor's trance. He turned and walked inside the tower. Located in a secluded corner, quiet, peaceful, the mural of Jahanara kneeling over Shah Jahan's tomb came into view. The mural occupied a wall which would have been easily missed unless someone was searching for it. Saima ran her hands over the faded unreadable Persian script at the bottom of the mural.

"Can anyone know about this?" Narayan Shastri pointed to the script.

"Yes, I can, it says that this paitining is made by Princess Jahanara and she scripted here as, "After his death, Mughal Empire will not be the same as it was...and I am giving him back everything...whatever I have received from him." A thin local old guide with a slight hunch stepped forward.

Saima turned gently to face the man.

Narayan and Saima looked at each other. There was a bright smile on Saima's face.

"Could we spend some time here…just the two of us? We would like to take a closer look at this mural," Shastri requested of the head of the group.

"Of course," the portly man replied. He guided the other ASI officials out of the room.

Earlier, in the car, Saima had deduced since Jahanara was the apple of Shah Jahan's eye, there existed a strong possibility the secret of the Noor was revealed to her. The script, which Saima had scribbled down on her pad, provided concrete evidence.

"You were right, Saima," Narayan stepped closer to the mural.

Major Rathore caught the curious stare of tourists as they followed the US ex-President and his wife through the lawns of the Taj Mahal. Though no one recognized the President, they were still curious to know who were this elderly couple guarded by security. The Major could hear soft murmurs as they made their way through the thin crowd of tourists to the marbled monument: *Must be some industrialist…Is that Warren Buffet…Looks like a Hollywood actor of yesteryears…VIPs have the best life.* The ex-President and his wife made their way to the marble mausoleum.

Narayan and Saima let their eyes take in the Jahanara mural at Musamman Burj. Unlike the intricate artwork and the precious stones at the marbled tower, which betrayed its centuries-old age, the mural looked frayed and jaded.

"Though it looks lacklustre, I feel it only adds to the enigma of the woman in black," Saima stated.

"I agree."

Saima continued to gaze at Jahanara's image. "Since the Mughal Dynasty fell into terminal decline after the rule of Aurangzeb, I think we can safely assume that the sacred stone did not pass from Shah Jahan to Aurangzeb," Saima repeated the Persian script, "*After his death, Mughal Empire will not be the same as it was.*"

Narayan nodded, "I too find it hard to believe that the emperor would have passed on the diamond to a son who imprisoned him and ordered the execution of his eldest son. Jahanara is the key."

"The question now is what did Jahanara do with it?" Saima wondered aloud.

Narayan tried to piece all of the clues together, "Object No. 27, our first clue was a part of Sher Mandal – Humayun's observatory. The object led us to Lodi Gardens, which turned out be a dead end. Our next concrete lead was this wall mural, engraved inside Musamman Burj..."

Saima gazed at Narayan and tried to follow his line of thought. "Narayan, where are you going with this?"

"The one common factor which links all our clues together is that they belonged to observatories and towers which the Mughals built."

"So you mean to say that the Noor is in some Mughal structure?"

"Exactly. If I were to make an educated guess, I would say that it was a structure built by Shah Jahan," Shastri'e eyes ran through the Persian script. "Saima could you repeat the script aloud for me once again," the professor requested.

"Sure... After his death, Mughal Empire will not be the same as it was...and I am giving him back everything...whatever I have received from him." Saima repeated the script slowly.

"And I am giving him back everything...whatever I have received from him," Narayan repeated. "And I am giving him back everything...whatever I have received from him," Narayan repeated once again. With his arms crossed across his chest, and his right hand stroking his chin, he stepped back from the wall and walked out to the main hall. The Taj came into view. Saima's anklets rustled and drew nearer. The professor's phone began to buzz.

"Hello...Major Rathore...we have good new....What!" Narayan's face contorted to a serious grim. "Okay...okay...," The professor disconnected his phone.

"Is everything all right?" Saima enquired.

The professor did not know what to say, he could not articulate.

"Narayan...," Saima placed her hand on Professor's shoulder.

Narayan's mind was in overdrive. A deluge of information swept through his conscious state. He tried to channelize it but it ran wild. The phone call from Major Rathore had opened the floodgates. As the tumult of information grew louder, Narayan closed his eyes, in an attempt to shut his mind off. And that's when it struck him. *Taj Mahal...built by Shah Jahan... I am giving him back everything...whatever I have received from him...*The professor opened his eyes.

"There's a...bomb..." Narayan put together a sentence.

"Where?" asked Saima concerned.

Narayan pointed his finger in the distance, "Taj...Taj Mahal..."

Saima's eyes grew wide in horror.

"We have…to leave…now…"

Major Khan, who was in disguise, strolled through the perfectly manicured lawns which led to the Taj Mahal. On his previous visit, he had a beard; today he had a long moustache topped with a hat. It seemed like any other day at the tourist destination. People wandered about, some serious, some happy, some in love. Major Khan felt that he was probably the only one present here who had an intention of destroying the eternal symbol of everlasting love. He looked at the white mausoleum; for a brief moment Major Khan felt a pang of remorse for what he was about to do. His hands shook, his breathing got shallow. Major Khan stopped for a second in order to get a hold over himself. As he looked at the monument once again, he noticed the DIA officers in the distance, outside the red mosque adjacent to the Taj Mahal. Captain Veer and Major Rathore looked like two black specks at the foot of a red hill. Major Khan took out his phone.

Captain Veer and Major Rathore were standing outside the Taj Mahal Mosque. The dignitaries had visited the marble mausoleum and were now inside the red sandstone mosque that stood adjacent in the courtyard. The US ex-President had requested the two DIA officers for a few minutes of privacy with his wife inside the mosque. Sensing no threat, Captain Veer agreed. Besides, their personal bodyguards would be inside the mosque.

Captain Veer was a little surprised when his phone vibrated in his pant pocket. He removed his phone and looked at the screen. It was an unknown number. The officer answered. "Captain Veer…"

"I must say you look no less than a film star in your suit."

"Major Khan?" Captain Veer had a grimace on his face.

Major turned to look at his partner.

"Yes. Correct. You recognized my voice. How nice of you. These days even friends do not recognize each other on the phone."

"What do you want? I don't have time to waste talking to scum like you."

"I see that. I have a simple request. Tell the US ex-President not to leave the mosque. If he does, he will leave this earth as well."

Captain Veer tensed and looked around. Major Rathore stepped closer to his partner.

"Last time was a hoax. This time I mean business. Look to your left."

Captain Veer saw a clean-shaven youth in a secluded corner of the riverfront terrace. The youth unzipped his cotton jacket discreetly to display wired explosives in the form of square plastic containers.

"One false move and the bomber will blow himself up."

Major Khan had a smile on his face, "Explosives have been planted in and around the Taj. If you want to see tourists walk out alive, follow my instructions. One false move and the Taj Mahal is history."

"What do you want?" Captain Veer's fist clenched.

"Release Mohammed Sayyed, who was arrested for planning the Delhi blasts."

"That will not happen."

"Then make it happen," retorted Major Khan. "Wait for my instructions…"

"Hello...hello...,"

The line went dead. Captain Veer looked at Major Rathore with a tense expression, "Call Narayan".

Narayan and Saima half-walked half-ran across the landscape of Agra Fort.

"Are the officers okay?" Saima enquired; her breath sharp and heavy.

"I think so...By the way, the diamonds...," Narayan took a deep breath, "They are at the Taj Mahal."

"How...?"

"Mughal structures..are the common factor...If the diamond...was given to Jahanara...then she would have hidden it at the Taj Mahal...the final resting place of her father and mother."

The duo rushed the group of ASI officials. The portly figure wondered what the rush was all about.

Narayan and Saima got into the car and drove away. Their destination – Taj Mahal.

20

A look of surprise crossed the professor's face as he and Saima walked towards the Great Gate. There was no sense of urgency or panic in the air, everyone moved at their own pace, there was no heightened security. *Maybe no one knows about the explosives.* As the two stepped through the Great Gate and entered Charbagh, the gardens, the professor again observed that life went about in a normal way. Tourists wandered about, guides were educating their group about the history of the place, security guards moved around nonchalantly. When Narayan looked at the mausoleum, he saw movement: security guards were cordoning the Taj Mahal and its expansive riverfront terrace.

Major Rathore had instructed the head of security to cordon off the area to tourists. Major Rathore hoped that Major Khan would not thwart the idea. There had been no further communication from the Major Khan. Captain Veer communicated the gravity of the situation to the US ex-President and urged him to remain inside until they resolved the situation.

The reason why Major Khan did not raise any objection to the security cordon was because he noticed Narayan making his way to the Taj. If Prof. Shastri was heading to the marble mausoleum, it probably meant that the diamond was in its vicinity. Major Khan began following Shastri discreetly though the thin crowd, making his way to the marble mausoleum as well.

Narayan reached the security cordon. "Sorry...no tourists allowed inside today," a guard informed Professor. The professor's phone rang, it was Major Rathore.

"Yes, Major Rathore."

"Narayan here, look to your left."

Narayan saw the officer who was a few yards away from the Taj, in the vicinity of the mosque.

"Direct the guard's attention to me," instructed the Major over the phone.

Narayan informed the guard, who had a curious expression on his face, as he turned to look at the DIA officer. Major Rathore gestured the guard to let Narayan and Saima inside the cordon.

Saima had been silent for a while now. A sense of inner turmoil was evident on her face, which Narayan failed to read. The professor's mind was busy unravelling the web that surrounded Noor-e-Jahan.

Footsteps gently echoed across the hallowed chamber of the Taj Mahal. The professor and Saima entered the chamber. For a moment, Saima's recurring dream, of the prince and his courtesan transforming into doves and flying away flashed across her eyes. Narayan, on the other hand, was firmly rooted in the present. He scanned each wall, each pillar, and each jali screen looking for a clue, looking for a sign that will light the path to the diamond and show him the way.

Major Khan, with his long moustache and hat, flashed a fake DIA id card to a guard in the security cordon outside the mausoleum. The guard saluted and let Major Khan through.

Major Rathore noticed a mustachioed man walking through the cordon. No one, except professor Shastri and Saima Azmi were supposed to be allowed through. He wondered who the man was. The Major started walking towards the mausoleum.

Saima, dressed in a black cotton pullover and black denims, cast a forlorn look as she sat besides Shah Jahan's cenotaph. Her mind was in a state of flux. When Narayan's eyes fell on Saima sitting at the tomb, his breath was taken by its resemblance to Jahanara's mural. The woman dressed in black, the enigmatic look which did not reveal what was running through her mind, the emperor's tomb...Narayan felt a sense of disbelief. And that is when it struck the professor, the location of Noor-e-Jahan, it was right in front of his eyes. Soft sounds of footsteps echoed; Narayan turned; Major Khan entered the chamber stealthily with a gun in his hand: a silencer.

The professor had a puzzled look on his face. Major Khan moved towards Narayan. Saima got up and stood next to the professor.

"Professor Shastri...where is the diamond?"

It took a few seconds for Narayan Shastri to connect the dots. "Major Salim Khan…?" he enquired.

"Yes…now tell me where the Noor-e-Jahan is located…and don't try to raise an alarm, otherwise…," Major Khan raised his gun.

Narayan adjusted the frame of his spectacles, "If you think you can intimidate with your revolver, think again."

"Well then," Major Khan trained his gun away from the professor and aimed it at Saima, "I may not be able to initimidate you, but if you will not tell where Noor-e-Jahan is, your companion gets it right between her eyes. My aim is very good, believe me."

Seconds ticked away on Major Khan's wristwatch. He pulled the trigger; Narayan froze. The bullet flew past Saima and hit a wall behind her.

"Professor, next time the bullet will find its mark," Major Khan grunted and tighthened his grip on the trigger gently pulling it.

Narayan took a deep breath, "Based on the clues, I would have to say that the diamond is here," Narayan pointed at Shah Jahan's tomb.

Major Khan and Saima looked at the tomb simultaneously.

"You are bluffing me…" Major Khan now had both his hands on the gun.

"No, I am not. There is a mural at the Musamman Burj, of Jahanara Begum sitting at Shah Jahan's tomb. At the base of the mural is a Persian script which says…After his death, Mughal Empire will not be the same as it was…and I am giving him back everything…whatever I have received from him…Shah Jahan passed on the Noor to Jahanara, his first born and favourite. When her father passed away, Jahanara gave him back everything he had given her, including the Noor. The diamond is inside the tomb."

Major Khan took one look at the tomb, then at Narayan Shastri, "Thank you professor, that will be all…," Major Khan fired his gun.

The bullet should have penetrated Narayan's flesh; instead, it hit Saima. Saima had moved in front of Narayan as Major Khan fired his gun. Narayan caught hold of Saima's falling body. Major Khan's grip on the gun loosened, it fell to the floor. He uttered a name, "Safi…"

21

Safi Khan could not believe her luck when she found the old Bairam Khan letter in an antiquated almirah in the storage room. She could not resist the sense of adventure that had come calling. Safi had decided to find out more about the 'Key of Fortune' and the mystery stone mentioned in the letter. Her architectural college in London was arranging a trip to Delhi and Safi decided to be a part of the trip. She had not informed her brother about the letter or about the trip. The sister would tell her brother only if she could get her hands on the Key of Fortune. It would be a nice surprise.

Once in Delhi, Safi began to visit libraries to read up on Bairam Khan, and began to visit various historical structures of the Mughals. She was supposed to go with her group on a city tour on the day of the blasts, but decided instead to spend time at a library. When the blasts happened, Safi realized that she had been proclaimed dead by the authorities. The architecture student viewed this as an opportunity to stay back in Delhi and continue searching for the Key of Fortune. Little did she realize the impact the news of her death had on her brother back in Pakistan.

She stumbled upon Object No. 27 as the Key of Fortune while she was reading a historical tome about Mughal relics in museums. The object was part of the display at Purana Qila museum in New Delhi. Safi immediately notified her mother, and then called her brother.

Major Khan came to New Delhi with a fake passport. He had come to the city with a secret mission: to blow up the Taj when the US ex-President visited. This was a secret he had not revealed to Safi.

Major Khan bribed a high-ranking official – the portly figure – at the ASI to get him Object No. 27. Major Khan and Safi tried hard to decipher the object but could not make progress. Major Khan's well-placed sources informed him that two DIA officers were planning to take help from a history professor to track him and the object. Safi Khan became Saima Azmi to unlock the mystery of the diamond – Noor-e-Jahan.

22

Safi lay in the hands of professor Shastri. The bullet had pierced her left lung. Major Rathore entered the chamber and immediately took out his service revolver, "Hands in the air!" he pointed his gun at the Major Khan, who stood motionless. Major Khan removed his fake moustache and hat.

Major Rathore's eyes grew wide, "Major Khan! Your hands in the air now."

Major Khan simply slouched to the floor.

Major Rathore called for backup and an ambulance.

Narayan's eyes turned moist. He was gently stroking Safi's forehead.

"Nara..yan...I am sorry...I did...not know...about the bomb...."

"Don't worry, don't waste your breath...the ambulance will be here soon."

Safi smiled weakly, "This is my last breath."

"Don't say that," Narayan interjected.

"My dream came true after all," Safi looked into Narayan's eyes. She could see twin reflections of herself on his spectacles: Safi and Saima. "I just wish I could fly away with you like the prince and his courtesan did in the dream. Like doves..."

Narayan hugged Saima. She was motionless, her blood spread across the professor's cream sweater. Narayan looked at Saima, her breathing had stopped. He continued holding her.

Major Khan was numbed. He did not how to deal with the fact that he had shot his own sister, the one person most precious to him.

Captain Veer ran into the chamber. He stopped when he saw the blood and the motionless body of Saima.

Major Khan got up and stood weakly. The two officers had their revolvers pointed at him.

"I have killed my own sister, Safi...." Major Khan cried loud. Before anyone could react, Major Khan shot himself. Red blood drops sprayed across the white walls of the chamber and stained its floors. The two officers lowered their guns and tried to catch their breaths. Narayan Shastri held the limp figure of Safi in his hands. Her blood seeped deeper across the professor's cream sweeter.

The afternoon sun sat high in the sky. Tourists were still wandering across the gardens; some wondered why the mausoleum had been cordoned off.

Major Khan did not seem like a normal man as he made his way across the riverfront terrace. He did not look like a man who had any control of his movements. Major Khan resembled a puppet whose strings were pulled by an unseen force, like a kamikaze pilot. Major Rathore and Captain Veer closely followed Major Khan.

The youth, with explosives strapped to his chest, came out of nowhere, taking the two officers by surprise and rushed towards Major Khan. Major Khan, calmly, caught the youth and pinned him to the ground.

Captain Veer captured him from Major Khan and handed him over to security personnels. Professor Shastri removed Major Khan's jacket, his fake moustache and hat and came out from Major Khan's disguise. Major Rathore instructed DIA personnel to scan Charbagh garden for explosive devices.

Outide the mausoleum, tourists continued to take in the sights of the Taj Mahal. Life continued as normal.

Epilogue

Professor Shastri gazed out of the window. A tree outside the window had spots of yellow flowers across its bare brown branch, a sign that summer was not far away. A warm breeze blew across; winter had thawed into spring. The professor, dressed in a full sleeve formal shirt and denims sat in his office. A soft knock rasped on his door.

"May we come in," Captain Veer entered the room and stood at the door along with Major Rathore.

Prof. Shastri smiled, "Yes, please."

"It has been a while," Major Rathore took his seat followed by Captain Veer.

"It has been a while," replied Prof. Shastri.

"How have you been?" Captain Veer enquired.

The professor was silent.

"Why did you not allow us to reveal your identity," Major Rathore changed the topic, "to the media and the public? You are a hero. You prevented a terrorist attack."

"I simply figured the location of the Noor," Professor Shastri replied, "which will never be substantiated anyway." The professor looked out the window, "I don't think Shah Jahan's tomb will be dug up anytime soon. Even if the biggest diamond ever known to humankind is in it," he paused. "You guys are the real heroes. Besides, I value my privacy too much to reveal my identity in the public sphere."

"Hmm...I can understand," Captain Veer replied. The Captain looked at his partner. Major Rathore nodded his head. Captain Veer removed a large orange envelope and kept it on the Professor's table.

"We may need your help, once again," Major Rathore leaned forward.

Narayan stared at the envelope.

The Noor-e-Jahan was history.